Child of Satan

Child of Satan

Kevin Laymon

ISBN 978-0-578-41401-0

Printed in the United States of America

First Printing, 2019

Edited by Danielle Fisher

Published by Ikigai Publishing ™

www.AuthorKevinLaymon.com

www.Twitter.com/Kevin_Laymon

www.Facebook.com/AuthorKevinLaymon

www.Instagram.com/Kevin_Laymon

Child of Satan is dedicated to daughters and sons.
Aspire to be better.

I will tell you this, oh sweet brother...
You will need to tap into Father's rage
if you wish to complete his task

Table of Contents

Part One
A Father's Demand

A blast of fire wreathed a quarter-dozen lost and wandering souls. Their cries of agony and despair were eternal. Salvation was no longer an option. The warped hands of a broken clock lied to all who listened. Believing that one could be saved from this place of torment was about as foolish as kissing the feet of a plagueborn rat on the hour of sickness spreading.

Dressed in a black cloak with minor golden accents embroidered throughout, a man wandered through the ravine of red bedrock and flame. The fires burned for as far as the eye could see. Soot and ash rose up from over the distant horizon, and the scent of sulfur lingered beneath a sky of stone. The man's hair was shoulder length and snow white. It wavered in the breeze of smoke as he continued to press forward in his journey up along the ravine. His eyes were black like the nightward sky that was barred from ever arriving on the shores of these lands. The sun never shined here, and the moon was as much a fable as pixies and pirates were to a twelve-year-old in search of purpose in a world beyond his doorstep. The man's face was pretty and his pale skin was soft, yet ashy. Beneath his cloak, he wore a mixture of black leather and wool. Much like his cloak, golden accents were stitched into the clothes and the man was dressed finely on this hour of chaos and despair.

Men and women reached out from nearby pockets of stone. Imprisoned for eternity, they clawed out through fire and smoke. They whispered silently - directly into the man's mind.

Take me, they called. *Ravage me,* they beckoned. *Break me*, they pleaded. *Claim me*, they offered. *Free me,* they desired.

The man's name was Victor. He was unmoved by the pleas for freedom - these offers of sexual conquest in exchange for a glimpse into something greater. Victor was a vampire, and the very first of his kind. Born to the circle of lust, he was a child of Satan, and perhaps one of the fallen angel's greatest creations.

Eternal war had plagued the nine hells since before the dawn of time, and lust was the great unifier. Victor had been raised in the front lines of conflict. He had grown into a man who was well to do with both seduction and sword. He had slain countless devils, demons, imps, and even an abyssal tyrant. There had been prophecies told of a time when a son would unify the sixteen warring factions. Under the banner of Satan, the nine rings would pour out from their prison and the battle for eternity would begin.

Time was unending in the nine rings. There were no days or months or festivals or years. It was only fire and brimstone: agony and pain forever. Despite these truths, the prophecy had- at last- come true, and God's seals were in the process of being broken. Devils and demons marched to war under Satan's command, and the greater war was well underway.

Victor continued to walk up the ravine. His eyes were dead and hollow without emotion. His eyebrows were stiff and unmoving. He reached the peak of the chasm and then caught sight of something towering in the distance.

Standing with its back arched over a rocky ledge, a creature gazed into a lake of blood and rot beneath the stone shelf. Shards of glass and rock poked through the monster's red, leathery skin. A trio of heads twisted and writhed from the beast's backside. One of a great red dragon scowled with a glare that could cut through stone. Smoke and heat billowed from the lizard's flared nostrils. The second head was of a child. A mere infant, the newborn had a sour face and often cried from its tomb of anguish. The third head was of a black ram. Two great horns curled up over its head and poked into the beast's backside. The animal's expression was stagnant and of disgust. A collection of fresh wounds and scars ran above the area where the antlers kissed the skin. Even with an arched back, the red-skinned monstrosity was colossal. It turned to face the son with its main head. A collection of shadow and chaos cackled across its broken skin, and the image of its true face was distorted. It growled with a deprived tone, and as it did, shadows seeped from every pore of its skin. Coated with a blighted phlegm, its voice was lost to the agony of thought, for living in this prison of darkness took its toll on all creatures, even the mightiest of evil: the lord Satan himself.

The breathing avatar of my father, Victor thought. *Each of the nine hells has one, but this is the only one that I've ever known.*

".dlihc ym, drawrof petS," the essence cackled from the shadows.

Victor silently glided forward as was commanded of him. His body crumpled into a kneeling position. With his back arched, he buried his chin into his chest and gazed to the coarse stone floor below. Gargoyles glared up into his eyes from their tomb of stone. Frozen in time, these damned souls harbored a haunting stare. Victor's eyes remained heavy and still as he gazed back into the faces of stone. He listened to his father's whispers. He would nod from time to time, but he never lifted his head or questioned his feral calling.

The beast growled in pain and Victor lifted his eyes to watch his father tear into his own belly. Satan plunged a pair of fingers into the fresh wound. The beast seethed in anger and its draconic head blew fire out across the sky of stone. A loud crack echoed across the cavern as a river of blood flowed between its fingers. The infant squealed, and the ram let out a sharp bleat. Satan tore forth a rib from his side.

".legna eht fo ylleb eht otni ti egnulp dna uoy otnu bir siht ekaT"

The great beast discarded the broken bone to the floor. It slid to a stop before Victor and the son bowed in total silence.

".snevaeh eht ruoved dna htrae eht morf tuo deelb yam ew taht os nekorb si laes lanif eht erofeb enalp latrom eht no covah kaerW .nos ym ,og woN"

The beast lifted its back and straightened its posture. Agony, unbound, hissed from every corner of its broken body. The dragon snipped at the child and the ram groaned. A great and mighty cock wavered between the beast's naked legs. The fallen angel wrapped his fingers around his enormous, red shaft. He then began to stroke at his tool for pleasure. Halting in his movement, the monstrous red giant froze. Squeezing the organ tightly, his eyes rolled into the back of his skull and he let out a groan that quaked the earth beneath Victor's feet. The mighty organ began to vibrate and twitch- suspended between the fingers of its owner's grasp. A burning fire ruptured from the head and sprayed along the stone walls of the cavern beside Victor. The bedrock sizzled under the fury of an inferno onslaught and a passage was carved into the stone. The beast released his grip and then a harsh collection of squeals and screams cut through the air like daggers to the flesh of a newborn. Victor's belly writhed in anguish as he endured kneeling before a dispersion of total anger and hate. Shadows washed over him before whistling through the air and seeping into the cracks along the stone sky.

Victor lifted his head. His father was gone and he was left kneeling along the edge of the volcanic fissure. Victor stood and turned to face the fresh corridor to his right. Lava dripped from the newly cut stone. He threw back his ebony cloak. He then rested the palm of his hand against the cold steel hilt of a blade that remained sheathed at his side. Turning back towards the great ravine ahead, he glanced down upon rivers and lakes of liquid fire. Cradled between the unending flames was a great pool of blood and rot. The inferno runneth over the crimson lake like a chalice overfilled, and a legion of devils and imps spawned forth from the festering pools like wasps being born of a kicked nest. They marched through the endless caverns, chanting to the tune of an ambient and ghoulish song.

The fourth seal had been broken, and Satan's forces were marching to war. The assault on the mortal plane was well underway, but heaven was the true and ultimate prize: the fabled flag to be captured by the legion of evil and hate.

The scent of pine lingered in the air. A mixture of sap and needles and fresh tasting wind; the perfume was enigmatic and all too specific. Lilith was near.

"So," a feminine voice cut through the air from behind Victor. "What's the play?"

Victor didn't bother turning to face the caller. He knew the girl well, and through his conflicted medley of thoughts, he had no times for his sister's games.

Shadows hissed through the air and then the girl appeared before Victor. She was naked from head to toe. Her black hair draped her pale skin like silky curtains that reached down below her buttocks. She also had a ponytail that was pulled back behind the crown of her head. A pair of small, black horns protruded from behind her hair. Her figure was curvy and her face was pretty. Both of her pale arms were lined with scars. Eying a black cross necklace hanging from his sister's neck, Victor reflected on a time when he had asked his sister about the symbolic jewelry.

"I like it," she had once said. "He died for our sins, you know," she had toyed. She always loved to play games of darkness.

Ink bled from Lilith's inner iris as she stared at her brother through the veil of a condescending grin. This wasn't Lilith's true form. Victor had never seen his older sister as she really was. She disguised herself as sinners and saints. She often wore the skin of famous women: taken directly from the bindings of history's greatest books. This black-haired figure was often the persona that

Lilith took before her brother. Victor often wondered who the woman was that his sister was impersonating.

There was no time for questions on this day, though. His father had tasked him with killing the guardian angel Ariel. He was to travel to the holy city of Astra' Kandra: one of the last tributes to God on the mortal plane. He was to find the angel and plunge the rib fragment into her belly. Once dead, the angel would ascend to heaven, but with the broken bone lodged in her belly, she would be impregnated and a child would be born into the heavens.

"You can't go to the mortal plane dressed like that," Lilith snickered. Her tone was soft and seductive.

Lilith snapped her fingers. The sound cut through the air and echoed through the cavern. A heap of Clothing appeared before her, and Victor blinked his eyes. Before he could reopen his lids, Lilith was fully dressed. She now wore a black, lace corset top that was stitched into a dress skirt bottom. Her pale arms were lined with ebony leather straps and bracelets. She bit into her lower lip. Blood was quick to run, and Victor lowered his eyes as he tried to ignore the luscious scent. Lilith turned the blood into lipstick. Her puffy lips were now a seductively strange deep purple. The ink that bled from her eyes clung to her skin like eyeliner. She smiled. Within seconds, she was fully clothed. The upper half of her hair was pulled back with a lacy black hair tie. The lower half was still draping down her backside. Her false appearance was only disguised further by use of leather, lace, and blood.

"How did you know that I was going to the surface world?" Victor's eyes drifted over to meet his sister as he broke his silence for the first in many years. The eye contact brought a smile to the surface of the girl's cynical expression.

"I was listening to you and Father speak."

Of course you were, Victor thought. *You are always listening.*

"Mortals and men dress in linens and rags, my sweet brother. Only princes and kings dress in the finer variety of garments."

Victor was far from kindled with his sister's presence. He

didn't hate her, but he also didn't love her. She was often a nuisance. Always watching and commenting, she often whispered maddening thoughts unto her silent brother. She reveled in many pleasures, but tormenting her younger brother was one of her favorite things.

"Well," Lilith's voice trailed off before returning full circle with a hate-induced tone of chaotic excitement. "You are a *prince*, I suppose."

Victor turned to walk away.

"At least alter the appearance of your eyes, my dear brother" the girl hissed. "It's a tell of your origin, and the mortals will see through it for the beautiful stain that it is."

Victor pressed his eyelids together. He then rolled his eyes back into his skull. The skin above the oculars twitched for a moment as his mind slipped into a seizure for a fraction of a second. He then rolled the eyes back into place and reopened his lids. His eyes were now a ghastly blue. They glowed softly under the reflection of light that the distant fires offered.

"Better?" He spat, glancing back towards Lilith.

"I'd fuck you," his sister hissed.

Victor lifted his upper lip. There were no limits or lines to Lilith's comments or desires. Victor had been born to the circle of lust. He was the son of the allfather and Satan had impregnated the embodiment of desire so that such a monster may be birthed. Despite this truth, Lilith was Satan's first child. She had traits from all of the nine hells. Her chaotic reach was vast, and her necrotic grip ran deep into the flesh of sanity.

Victor returned his gaze to the freshly cut stone. His newfound eyes analyzed the corridor ahead. It was the passage that would lead him to the surface world. An ambient static flickered and warped the air before him. Dimensions were colliding and imploding within the open cavern ahead.

"Father's magic can be strange sometimes," Lilith commented as Victor stepped forward towards the veil of crackling energy.

The vampire broke through the wave of static. He could feel

his mind collapse beneath the weight of eternal chaos. No soul could walk such a path without being torn to pieces. Any mind would be fragmented to such torment, but Victor and his sibling were born for this, and so he endured the walk through turmoil and discord. His journey took him through sixteen planes in the blink of an eye. It felt like eternity. His skin bubbled and his mind boiled to the heat of the inferno. He was beginning to break, and his soul was nearing the brink of total annihilation. He pinched his eyes tightly shut and screamed. His voice was lost to the vacuum of a collapsing spacetime. He felt as though he could bear no more, but then a silence befell the air around him. He opened his eyes to find himself standing in a cavern. The air was cold and lacked scent. The way back was sealed shut.

Faces and bodies, twisted and warped amongst the stone - immovable yet seemingly always watching - lashed out at Victor via psychological means.

The vampire glanced into the stagnant eyes of an imprisoned soul. The gargoyle was completely motionless: a snapshot taken from a time of total agony and terror. He returned his gaze forward. He could hear the stone cry as the faces forced their gaze upon him.

Victor glided forward through the cavern. He traveled through limbo for hours and hours. The minutes bled into days and the minor scrapes of time ruptured into greater wounds. It felt as though the very fabrics of time had been broken. Minutes felt like days and days soon seemed like months, which became years along a linear path towards eternity.

Victor was suspended within limbo. Twirling through the air, he turned back to face the path leading from where he had traveled. The passage directly behind him was still sealed shut, and a wall of solid stone remained. He hadn't made it but two paces forward. Victor pressed the palm of his hand to the cold stone. He then turned about. The passage ahead had also been sealed shut. Glancing from left to right, Victor confirmed a difficult truth. He was sealed in a prison of stone. His eyes widened as he wrestled with the temptation of fear.

Limbo was a domain that belonged to Death, and Death was no friend to Satan. The faceless reaper had made a pact with God long ago. He was to harvest souls from the mortal plane and offer them to God for judgement. Often times, the reaper would find amusement in tormenting lost souls before offering them as tribute to the great man in the sky. Death's greatest weapon was the total disintegration of one's mind. Victor knew of the reaper's games. He also knew that Death despised the creator of man just as much as he abhorred the great beast below the mortal plane. It wasn't out of loyalty that the reaper served God, rather the pact that was made between the two patrons served to benefit the fallen angel. His loyalties were on loan and, as such, they could be bought and sold at any time.

The reaper was capable of imprisoning souls in this domain, and Victor was flirting with the idea of pledging himself to the fallen angel.

"He is foolish to dance with the prince of blood and lust," Lilith called. Her voice was muffled by a wall of solid stone. "Break him," she beckoned. "He will bow to you."

Victor knew better. The reaper would never bow to another, let alone a child of Satan. He instead closed his eyes and exhaled a breath of frigid air. Through total silence, he offered himself to the reaper and a pact was made between the two. Should a stalemate ensue between heaven and hell, Death would be granted a legion of obedient soldiers. Then the fallen angel could wreak havoc on the mortal plane and roll the dice in absorbing the dimension into his own stagnant domain.

A mystic fog swirled around Victor. The palm of an icy hand pressed against the center of the vampire's chest. The frigid hand ignored his skin, muscle and bone. It slipped through his shell and grasped at his beating heart. Victor's eyes widened and he gasped for air as the cold hand began to squeeze. Death's grasp was unmatched. It tore the beating heart from Victor's chest. Victor watched in horror as the essence of death whispered something in the finality of goodbye. The heart was insurance against deception. Victor would not only be granted passage to the mortal plane, but he would also be empowered with a false sense of immortality. With his heart now belonging to the reaper, his fate after life would also be decided by the cold whispers of Death.

A second hand reached out through the fog. The reaper extended a necrotic finger towards Victor's forehead. The limb was twisted and mangled. Much like the palm of his other hand, Death slipped through Victor's skin without forbearance. Victor could feel his sanity implode. It was a pain that ran deep. It was foreign and yet strangely familiar. It was toxic like power, and it coursed through his veins like fire before bleeding from his skin like shadow and smoke. Victor was left feeling weightless. His pulse was no more, and his skin was frigid and devoid of all life.

The fog lifted and the way forward was again open. Passage had been granted. Lilith appeared before her brother. She harbored an expression of disappointment. Victor's breathing was slowed as he began to walk forward without a pulse. The avatar of his sister dispersed into shadow as he stepped through her physical location.

"You can never betray him now," Lilith hissed as she reappeared further on ahead of her younger sibling. "He has claimed you, and Father wouldn't so much as lift a finger to save you."

Victor knew this. Deception was a trait that was all too common of demons and devils and the reaper knew it. Death could see through the veil of a lie, and the fallen angel was always true to his word. Should Victor ever go back on the deal, Death would chase him. Like a pack of feral wolves who never tire, the reaper would chase Victor to the ends of eternity. He would claim his soul and put it on display for all to see.

The vampire continued forward along the corridor of stone and Lilith glided backwards so the she could stay ahead of her brother.

"What does it entail?" She questioned softly, but the brother ignored his sibling. "You know he is hedging his bets against Father."

Victor knew this, too. Satan and God had been dancing

since the dawn of time, and Death had worked alongside God for far too long. Victor saw opportunity in doubt. He gambled with his soul and placed a bet that was ever in Death's favor. The war between heaven and hell was about to reach its climax, but when the dust settled, Death would find himself without purpose. The pact was a hedge against both heaven and hell. Victor and his sister were granted passage and the son was gifted with a stronger sense of vitality. In return, he would mark mortal souls. Once marked, men would be turned to follow Victor. They would come to know of immortality with restrictions. When those restrictions were met, they would succumb to Death's shadowy embrace. They would be barred from both heaven and hell, and Death's rein would begin.

Victor wondered what other deals the reaper was making behind God's back.

Suddenly, a flash of light flickered through the cavern and Lilith screamed as she was vaporized into liquid tar. Victor lifted his arms and shielded his face. The light blistered and burned his skin. Thinking quickly, he twirled his ebony cloak up over his face and knelt down to the ground so that he may be shielded from the burn of this inorganic light.

A stillness ensued.

Victor lowered his cloak and peeked his face out from behind the heavy veil of linen cloth. His face was blistered. A hissing steam seeped from the scorched lesions along his skin. The agony was endless. A black smoke bled from the cavern's stone and encased Victor like the waves of a colossal storm wreaking havoc on a sloop set to sea.

Victor closed his eyes.

The shadow's embrace was soothing to his fresh wounds. The lesions were sealed shut and his body returned to a state of wholeness. The gaseous shadow then dripped to the floor like liquid fire. The smoke twirled up into a vortex and Lilith was again reborn. She stared at her brother with a lifted brow and then offered a smirk before her eyes of ink went out of focus.

"The star of David," Lilith gestured towards the way back.

Victor spun around. The path was sealed shut and a star was scribed into the stone with a glowing light that radiated with a sense of divine power.

The sister grinned. "We have broken into the mortal plane."

Part Two
Welcome Party

The cavern beyond the Star of David opened up into a much larger cavity. This was the first time in their journey towards the surface world where the path ahead wasn't a dense and narrow passage. The ceilings ahead were vaulted and the walls grew distant. The extra space allowed for a sense of breathability and room, something that Victor was grateful to find.

Light appeared from the far end of the subterranean expanse. It leaked out from around a bend and cast shadows along the wall. Victor froze. His posture became tense and his eyes grew sharp as he watched the shadows dance along the hall. He sunk his hand into his cloak and wrapped his fingers around the hilt of his otherworldly sword.

"Relax, little brother," Lilith shot Victor a grin. The tone of her voice climaxed as she put on a false falsetto. "Seems our welcome party has arrived."

Victor remained stiff.

Lilith shed her clothes like skin. Her corset dress dissipated into shadow and smoke as it made contact with the cavern floor. Her bare body, in this form, was pale, curvy, and attractive. She radiated with a sense of sexuality and she straightened her posture as she strutted forward towards the light around the bend.

"No," Victor growled. "Go transparent," he ordered of his sister and she stopped to turn and face him with rolling eyes.

"You are no fun," she complained. Her bare nipples were stiff like stone. She hung her head like a child being refused a savory sweet. A noose appeared around her neck. She grabbed hold of the robe and playfully tugged. A crack echoed across the cavern as she rose up into the air and floated towards the ceiling. Her naked body shimmered as she went transparent. Only Victor could see her clearly now. He wished that he couldn't. She was always a distraction. She made a series of grunts and snorts as she jokingly hung in place from the noose.

Plated from head to toe, a pair of warriors crept through the cavern. Their chainmail jingled beneath their polished armor, and the shadows along the stone bowed before the presence of their roaring torches. The darkness withdrew deep into the cracks along the wall.

Victor watched as the two men drew near. They lifted their torches high above their heads and the light shown all around Victor. The vampire was illuminated and standing in place with a hand resting against his blade, Heart Cutter. He scowled. The warriors looked to one another and nodded. One of them whistled and then they both parted so that a third man could approach from around the bend. This man was shorter than the two guards. His back was arched and - with a limp - he shuffled forward beneath a tattered black robe. Lifting his head, he threw back his hood and glanced to Victor with a hollow expression. He was a man but - while oddly short and of small frame - he also had scaly skin that split and flaked as he forced a decrepit smile. All but his yellow eyes were slave to the grotesque skin condition. He revealed a mouth of rotting teeth as he wrestled with words and the overbearing stench of death wafted out from his mouth.

"Is it really you?" He forced through a phlegm-induced tone. His lips cracked and blood leaked from the fresh wound as he spoke. "A servant of the Dark Lord?"

Victor glanced to the guards before returning back to gaze upon the short, little monster. The guards avoided making eye contact at all.

"He is far more than a servant," Lilith choked out from above. She was still dangling from the noose. The mortals couldn't see her, and so they also couldn't hear her speak.

"I imagined you'd be," the scaly man's thought trailed off for a moment. "A bit more..."

Lilith kicked her feet. Her impersonation of a woman being hung was strikingly convincing. Victor continued to scowl. This was the first time that he had seen men who weren't subjects of his father's torment and madness. These men still walked on the mortal plane and their will was still their own.

"Anyway," the imp coughed into a clenched fist before he continued. "Our king has been eager to meet you in person. He has made the journey here so that he may lay eyes upon you and make a proper introduction." The imp reached into his robes and withdrew a small incense stick. Breaking the stick in two, he held one of the ends out towards one of the guards and blew on the twig. The wedge crumpled to dust and the guard inhaled: accepting the powder through his face and filling his lungs deeply. The imp then turned to the second guard and repeated the strange ritual before calling to Victor. "Come, come," he beckoned with a twisted and broken finger. "Let us go and meet the king of men."

Lilith dropped to the stone floor. Her body crumpled and her bones cracked. Her skin tore open and blood spurted from the fresh wounds. The three men were showered in a nonsensical amount of red liquid. Lilith was still transparent to them and only Victor could see the outlandish act. Just as soon as the blood began to drip from their armor and clothes, the crimson spray dissipated into smoke. Lilith's lifeless body twitched before she suddenly snapped her head back. Her neck was swollen and bruised, and she still wore the fake noose strap around her neck.

She forced a smile and Victor left her broken body on the floor as he followed the three men out towards the cavern exit.

Once outside, Victor was greeted by a clear twilight sky. He had never seen the sky before. Through tales he had heard of the endless abyss that hung above the mortal plane. Stars twinkled and Victor pondered on their origin and purpose. Tall, leafless trees swayed beneath a cool, crisp breeze and Victor welcomed the fresh tasting air with a deep breath.

The two guards and the imp approached a nearby caravan. A line of six horses stood behind the caravan and two more were strapped to the head of the wooden vehicle. Two more guards could be seen kicking around in the dirt beside the caravan. They appeared to be bored and without purpose, but as they saw Victor approach from out of the cavern, they straightened their posture and came to full attention.

"Just a moment," the imp excused himself. He climbed a pair of wooden steps and knocked against the vehicle's side. A door magically appeared and he entered. Candlelight leaked out into the air through the open entrance.

Left to himself, Victor looked towards the guards. They appeared to be mindless as they stared through him. He again looked to the sky. A full moon was illuminating the atmosphere beneath the stars. Bright and vibrant, the celestial body was beautiful, and Victor pondered on the fabled druids and elves who worshiped the planet like a deity. It was said that they still populated the forests of the mortal plane.

The imp exited the vehicle and climbed down the wooden stairs. He was followed by a much larger man. Draped in fine white silks and golden bits of jewelry, the larger man was heavyset and the caravan creaked under his weight as he exited behind the imp. He had a full beard of brown, coarse hair and his bushy eyebrows (of similar color) wormed across his upper brow as he walked. He shuffled forward with a sense of pride and grace. A vibrant neckpiece made of thick, golden plate hung around his flabby neck.

"I bet there is a sea of lard tucked behind that neck plate," Lilith called from behind Victor. She walked forward and stood by her brother's side. She had returned to taking on the form of her usual disguise. "Probably stinks of pocket sweat and the wet fur of a dying carcass, too. Fat scoundrel," she hissed. "I bet he opens nicely." She reached for Victor's sheathed blade. The vampire pivoted his hips and kept the weapon from his sister's reach.

The imp stopped before Victor. "May I introduce," he bowed and the large man's awkward stare was met with the vampire's ambient gaze. "The vanquisher, the conqueror, the righteous and noble, first of his name, Sir King Solomon: Tsar to all men.

"Tsar to all men," Lilith snickered. "There are many kings to man." She glided over towards the fat man and inspected him closely from head to toe. Victor watched her from where he stood before the king. "What makes *this one* so special?"

Despite his weight and size, the large man was glowing from head to toe with a sense of pride and charisma. His skin was clean and the aroma of a sweet flower, unbeknownst to Victor, clung to the man like a beautiful curse. His hair hung down beneath his big ears, and his soft stare was offered with bright, green eyes. He forced a smile. Behind his act of nobility and strength laid a sense of nervousness and doubt. Victor could smell it in the air. It was present and clear like the ambient sky that lay overhead.

The large man pressed the backside of his hand against the ridge of his mouth. A line of golden bracelets jingled along his forearm as he leaned in towards the imp and whispered something incoherent. The imp smiled and bowed once more before tossing a pair of fingers into the air and calling out to the guards standing back by the caravan. The two warriors were quick to shuffle over towards the line of standing horses. They untied one of the beasts. It was a great and mighty stallion whose body was chiseled of solid muscle from head to toe. Its coat of hair was black like the night sky, and small grey spots ran along the side of the great beast's pelt.

"A gift," the imp hissed. "From our true and noble king: Solomon, first of his name and heir to the kingdom of man."

The two guards offered the steed's reigns and Victor accepted the gift with a silent nod. The king then waved the guards away with a flick of his wide wrist.

"I have been eager to meet you," the king began. His tone was deep and the air bellowed from his lungs as he spoke. "Tell me, devil. Do you have a name?"

"Victor's eyes went in and out of focus as he watched his sister's madness. She was standing behind the king and she was blinking back and forth - shifting between projections. She impersonated Victor. The reflection was strikingly convincing. Her avatar had his clothes and hair, and she even wore his scowl as she withdrew his sword from her side. She then warped into the appearance of the fat king. She was portraying a scene with herself (as Victor) butchering herself (as Solomon). She played the role of both actors in the scene of blood and gore. She even mimicked the king's tone as she cried out and screamed in response of her belly being split open at the hands of her own projection. Victor was unamused.

"Victor," the son of Satan finally answered after an awkward delay.

"Well, Victor," the king forced a nervous smile. "Do you have a surname?"

Lilith returned to her usual form. She appeared again by her brother's side. "Lie to him," she said.

"Morgaf," Victor lied.

"It is such a pleasure to finally meet you, Victor Morgaf," the king said with a smile as he gently lowered his head. A bald spot could be seen at the crown of his round scalp.

"Likewise," Victor stated without emotion.

"It took us some time to acquire the Star of David," the king pardoned. "Please do tell the Dark Lord that we apologize for the delay come next you see him."

Victor said nothing, and the king again pressed the backside of his hand against the rim of his mouth. He leaned in towards the imp and whispered something once more. The imp shuffled forward.

"This gift, from our truly gracious king, is one of the finest purebreds in all of the seven kingdoms," he boasted.

Victor looked again towards the charger. It was certainly a magnificent beast: the embodiment of what a stallion should be from head to toe. Victor pressed a hand to the steed's face. The charger snorted a heavy breath of warm air. Its black coat was coarse and fine.

"His name is Midnight," the broken little man informed. "And I pray that he serves you well in your travels to Astra' Kandra."

"Pray," Lilith cried. "And whom do these men *pray* to, I wonder."

Victor threw back his cloak and pressed a hand to his sheathed weapon so that he may mount the horse without the sword's hilt injuring the steed. He rose up off the ground and glided atop the charger with an eerie silence, and the imp's eyes widened as he watched with enjoyment. Again, the king pressed his hand to his mouth and whispered something in secrecy to the imp. The short man then nodded.

"That's a fine blade," the imp hissed. "Was it forged in the fires of hell?"

Victor said nothing as he stroked the stallion's mane and adjusted his posture for riding.

"Perhaps you'd like to part with it," the imp implied. He writhed his hands together like a greedy little child who was about to dive into the depths of a savory meal. The skin on his hands cracked and bled in contact.

Again, Victor said nothing, and the king whispered down towards the imp once more.

"Surely we could offer an assortment of useful things for such a fine weapon," the imp offered desperately.

"They have no idea," Lilith scowled as she hunched down to the imp's eye level. She was still transparent to the mortals, but her presence forced the imp to stiffen his eyebrows. He could smell the lingering essence of her evil. He forced a gulp of air and looked back towards his king.

"This steed should be able to carry you to Astra' Kandra within a matter of days," the king embarrassedly shifted the conversation's focus. "One of my men will be waiting for you outside of the city gates on the dawn of the third morning," he informed. "From there, he will smuggle you into the city and then leave you to your work."

Victor nodded in silence before tightening his grip on Midnight's reins.

Lilith dropped her veil of transparency. She stood directly in front of the imp. She exerted a red glow from her hateful eyes as she rolled her neck loose before offering a menacing grin. The imp stumbled backward and tripped on something in the brush. Tumbling to the ground, he let out a cry and the king trembled, frozen in place.

The scent of a warm, salty liquid wafted through the breeze. The king had soiled his fine white linens. Victor silently cursed his supernatural sense of smell. He thought of it as a burden, at least on the mortal plane. Most men smelled of shit and pigs.

Pressing the heels of his boots into the steed's side, Victor relayed a command to the charger, and the horse took off with a tremendous burst of speed. The vampire was weightless and this lack of burden upon the steed only allowed for the magnificent beast to go faster and faster into the night. With the full moon positioned up over their right-hand side, Victor and Midnight cut through the leafless forest and rode far into the twilight. They had three mornings to reach Astra' Kandra and Victor had no interest in wasting time with mortals and men.

Part Three
The First Dawn

Victor rode straight through the witching hour with haste. He kept the moon over his right shoulder as he pressed eastwards towards dawn. Solomon was an adulterer, a delinquent, a scamp, and a liar. Despite these many truths, the king of men had been honest with Victor in regards to the tribute that he had offered the son of Satan. Midnight was as great a charger as any and the steed galloped at full speed for hours and hours without showing the slightest sign of exhaustion or fatigue.

The scent of crimson tugged at Victor's mind and he pulled back on Midnight's reins. The steed came to a stop and trotted in circles as Victor scanned through the darkness behind them. The horse kicked his back feet and neighed. Victor was thrown from the steed. He landed in the dirt with a grunt. Lifting his head, he caught sight of what had upset the horse.

Lilith had reappeared and she was hovering in the air before

Midnight. She lowered her heels to the earth. She was out of breath and gasping for air. Her face and hands were covered in blood. Victor stood to his feet. His black garments were tainted with a coating of loose dust.

"You weren't supposed to kill them," he growled.

Lilith said nothing. Her eyes softened as if she were ashamed for what she had done. A smile ruptured from a lifted cheek. She always was a bad liar.

"Father offered him a ring many moons ago," Victor said as he glided back up onto the horse.

"He still has it," his sister assured. "Or," she paused and offered a wider smile. "At least what's left of him."

Victor sighed and tightened his grips on the reins. Lilith then levitated up onto the horse and took a seat on the saddle behind her brother. She wrapped her arms around her sibling's waist and Victor scowled in silence. Pressing her face into her brother's backside, a bloody imprint was left stained into his cloak. She was exhausted from chasing after him for so long. Her pine perfume was blotched with the scent of iron as she exhaled a savory breath; the scent of blood was still strong on her tongue.

Victor flared his upper lip and then dug his heels into the horse. The steed took off once more and the trio continued their journey east together. Lilith was famished and this kept her mostly silent in their travels. It was something that Victor was grateful for, even if she had betrayed the king and devoured his flesh. Lilith licked the blood from her fingers as they rode in silence. She used her brother's cloak to scrub the crimson from her face, and when she was free of the stains, she sucked on the cloth and leeched all of the red from the fibers. A few hours went by. Dawn was breaking and the charger was still empowered with a strength that only a purebred lineage could offer.

The sun's rays shown out across the land like the cleansing waters of a high tide come to shore. The light was bright and Victor squinted his eyes. He had never seen the sun before and the world was very different under its shine. It pained his eyes to look towards the land beneath the sun's rays. The beams of light continued to wash over the land and the two children of Satan were bathed under the emanation. Lilith screamed and burst into shadow. Her gaseous form shimmered in the air as she reappeared screaming atop the horse.

"He knows that we are here!" She shrieked.

Victor's flesh was quick to blister and bubble. His sister's essence was withering away and he was soon to follow. The pain was unbearable and he couldn't help but cry out as his eyes searched through the bright light for shelter. A large wooden structure lie ahead. The light continued to sear his skin as he dug his heels deeper into the steed's side. Midnight unleashed a burst of speed as Lilith continued to squeal in agony. The scent of burning flesh followed the two children as they rode forward through the dawn of the morning sun. Victor could make out a sign that read *White Stag Saloon*. A stable could be seen beside the tavern where a half a dozen horses were tied to wooden posts.

Lilith was flailing about like a fish out of water and her movements served to hold the great steed back. Victor tugged at the reins and pressed his chest flat against the horse's neck. He shifted his weight to the right and Midnight made way towards the stables. Pulling back on the reins, the horse slowed, and Victor dived to the ground. He rolled to a stop beneath the line of foreign horses. The steeds were quick to frighten. They trampled Victor's broken body like a mouse. He grunted and yelped as he endured the hooved assault. Despite the pain, he was now free of the sun and his melted skin began to slowly mend.

Lifting himself to his feet, Victor pressed the palm of his right hand to his belly. One of the horses had cut deeply into him and - being weakened by the sun - it would take time for the wound to heal. Victor called out to Lilith. She was still riding Midnight and she was phasing in and out of her flesh. There was no solitude to be found in her ethereal form. The light cut through her disbursement of shadow just as it did her flesh-bound avatar.

Victor closed his eyes and pressed his left hand forward. He whispered out across the plains and spoke directly into the mind of the steed. Normally, he'd have to gaze into the eyes of a mildly intelligent creature in order to whisper into its mind, but animals were different. If he closed his eyes and focused, he was sure that he could throw his voice into the wind and penetrate the beast's mind through its ears. Navigating between the web of conflicting thoughts, he calmed the horse and beckoned for it to return.

Midnight came to a stop and began to trot in circles under the rays of the sun. He slowly galloped back towards the stable where Victor remained frozen in time. The son to Satan could feel the steed brush up against his hand. He opened his eyes to be greeted with a warm snort.

Lilith's dying body slid from atop the leather saddle. She crashed into the ground with a thump. She then burst into shadow, which seeped and squealed into the wooden cracks along the stable's wall.

Victor's breathing was sporadic. He stroked the horse's mane and buried his melted face into the charger's muscular side. His wounds continued to slowly heal. Lilith had been under the sun for longer. It would take time before she too could begin to mend. The sun's rays shimmered through the cracks along the stable's thin roof. One of the rays pierced through Victor's backside like a sharp dagger. He lifted his eyes to face the saloon. He paused to think for a moment before he called out to his sister. His voice was lost to the pain of melting chords.

"Lilith," he forced through a weakened tone. "We've got to get inside, Lilith."

Shadows bled from the cracks in the wood. Lilith's gaseous form took shelter beneath her brother's cloak. This notion of safety and asylum was a lie. Cloth couldn't save the two children from the light of the sun.

Victor wrapped the horse's reins around a wooden post and then knelt down to the ground. He dug between the loose straw and clenched a collection of pebbles and stone between his fingers. Slipping the rocks into one of his pockets, he then glanced up towards a gathering of clouds in the sky. He waited for the overcast, and when the sun's shine was softened, he lifted himself into the air and glided towards the tavern. Lilith tightened her grip around her brother and Victor's lungs were emptied of air. Even beneath the veil of cloth and clouds, the sun's rays were unwaveringly cruel. They served to be a great weapon that was cast down from the sky. Somehow, God had known about the arrival of Satan's children to the mortal plane. He had empowered the sun and barred the siblings from traveling under the light of day.

Victor wondered what else the self-proclaimed Allfather knew of their endeavor. *Does he know of our intentions? Is Astra' Kandra a trap waiting to be sprung?*

Reaching the tavern's entrance, Victor's feet made contact with the earth and he pressed his free hand against the door's latch. His skin bubbled and melted into the iron. He bit into his lower lip and tried to mask the pain as best he could as he entered the saloon and plucked his hand from the hot metal.

Victor quickly scanned through the tavern as he continued to disguise his agony. Anyone who looked upon his broken face would know that something was up. He could impose a false image into a simple mind, but he couldn't do this to more than one mind at a time. A trio of men sat around a wooden table in the corner of the saloon. One of them projected his insides through the open orifice of his face. He sprayed vomit out across the table before sliding from his stool and crashing against the cold stone floor. His two companions were so far gone that they paid him no mind at all. They were trying to play cards, but their grasp on reality was limited and they swayed beneath the tides of consciousness as they rocked from side to side atop their wooden stools with a broken, slurred speech.

"Filthy mongrels must've drunk straight through the night," Lilith hissed from her gaseous form. "They probably wouldn't even feel it if you were to gut them like the swine that they are."

Victor could feel his sister's eyes peering out from beneath his open cloak. He spotted a woman working behind the bar. She had blonde hair and fair skin. She was dressed in tattered linens and was scrubbing wooden mugs with a brown rag over a tin tub. She lifted her eyes to meet Victor across the room. He was quick to search for the iris of her eyes. Her green-eyed gaze was soft and welcoming. Victor was quick to impose his lie, and she was oblivious to the deception of agony. She offered a smile in total silence.

Open windows allowed for light to peer into the saloon. The rays were limited in their shine, and Victor avoided the pockets of illumination as he made his way towards the bar. Empty tables were clean and free of men and mugs. The lingering scent of lemon was fresh in the air.

"Welcome," the girl behind the bar said as Victor drew near.

Victor nodded and leaned against the wooden counter. He was weak and beginning to lose the strength to walk, let alone stand.

"What'll you have?"

"Any rooms available?" Victor fought out. It took all of his strength to keep up this deception. His body was writhe with agony.

The barmaid finished cleaning one of the wooden mugs and then set it out to dry along a dozen others. She then offered a second smile as she awarded the vampire with her full sense of attention.

"We've got common rooms that run one gold per night." She paused to giggle as she took note of the sun's shine that was trickling into the room. "Or day," she corrected. "And we've got private rooms that run two gold for a day's stay."

"Oh, let's share a room with the mortals," Lilith hissed. "I hear they fuck like monkeys and apes."

Victor stared directly into the barmaid's bright green eyes. The iris was a gateway into the mind, and through the sexual projection of lust and desire, Victor strolled through the open door, invited.

"I'll take a private room," he informed as he slipped a hand into his front, left pocket.

Maintaining his ghoulish stare, Victor withdrew three small pebbles from his pocket. Without voice, he whispered directly into the girl's mind. A second deception was laced into her head. He dropped the stones down onto the counter. With the vampire's will projected into the girl's mind, her eyes failed to see the rocks as they were; rather, she saw the stones as solid gold coins. She placed her fingers over the jagged stones and slid them off the edge of the bar where she caught them in the palm of her hand.

"Very gracious of you," she said as she slipped the pebbles into a pouch of gold coins. "Um, let's see here," she looked over towards a clipboard that was hanging from a rusty nail. With her gaze broken, Victor was cast out from her mind. "It looks like the third room is still open. It'll be the third door on the right of the head of the stairs. Would you like me to show you?"

"That won't be necessary. Is there a key?"

The barmaid rolled her lips inwards before answering. "Yeah, we stopped giving them out after a bunch of folks kept walking off with them. The doors lock from the inside though."

Victor said nothing as he turned to face the stairs in the corner of the room.

"My name's Joanna if you need anything." Her tone was soft and sweet. It was unlike the miserable wailers and sinners of the nine hells. This girl seemed genuine and kind. Victor hated her for it. He wondered how anything on this earth could be honest and pure. All of mankind were sinners. He figured that Joanna must've had demons in her closet. Maybe not the literal kind, but surely she had secrets of her own. He thanked her and made for the stairs.

Careful not to levitate, Victor climbed the stairs and approached the third door on the right. Light was seeping through the cracks along the bottom of the entrance. He wrapped his fingers around the latch and sighed. The door was unlocked and the light was quick to engulf Victor as he depressed the handle and proceeded inside into the room. Squinting and shrieking: blistering and burning, he leapt up into the air and levitated across the room and dove towards a window. He pulled off his cloak. The shadows of his sister dispersed and hissed as they bled into the cracks along the wall. He draped the cloth over the window frame. The room went dark, but Victor could still feel the light's presence. Turning to face a bookshelf, he tugged at the furniture and slid it in front of the window. A book fell from the shelf, and with the light now vanquished, he knelt down to pick up the tome.

Macbeth, by William Shakespeare, Victor read the title in silence.

"Shakespeare?" Lilith squealed. "Did you know that he was an indirect servant to Father?" She was commenting from the cracks along the wall. "His king was loyal to Father, and Shakespeare followed his king blindly until his dying days." Victor could sense her amusement. With her body broken, she would stay hidden so that she could heal throughout the day. "He transcribed the modern-day rendition of the Bible," she snickered. "Slipped a few good lines in there, too."

Victor placed the book back on the shelf and then glided over towards the room's single entrance. He engaged the lock on the door. Glancing above, he spotted a thick wooden beam that ran from one end of the ceiling to the other. He unfastened his belt and leaned his sheathed sword against the wooden bookshelf. His father's broken bone fragment hung from the belt. Its weight was surprisingly heavy. He then levitated up into the air and spun around so that he could slip the bridge of a booted foot up over the beam. Once in place, he planted the second foot alongside the first. He relaxed his shoulders and posture. Hanging freely upside down, he swayed in the air as he unbuttoned his white, Victorian shirt. His skin was muscular and toned yet scarred and broken. He exhaled softly as he scrunched up his face in pain and unfastened the final button. It wouldn't take Victor long to succumb to a deep, dead slumber. It was through sleep that his body could heal. He figured that by nightfall, his body would once again be whole and without laceration.

Part Four
Bloodbath

Victor fought through the murky waters of a hazy dream. The scent of iron tugged at his mind and beckoned him forward through the shadows. It demanded attention in a mysterious sort of way and called out to him with his father's words. He opened his eyes to find himself hanging over a bed at the White Stag Saloon. The sun had set and the cool air beyond the open window was blowing in from beneath the veil of a silk curtain. The moonlight peeked in and kissed the vampire on the left cheek. The soft glow was about all that he could bear in terms of light on his skin. His eyes shifted in and out of focus as he battled with the overwhelming scent of feast and famine.

The room below Victor was littered with corpses. Entrails and blood caked the walls like fresh paint to wood. Red liquid dripped from the ceiling at a sporadic rate, and Victor's eyes widened as he came to the realization of where exactly he was.

The scene of gore would be a normal accessory found within the depths of hell, but here - on the mortal plane - humans were to wear their insides *beneath* their skin.

Victor could sense the presence of his sister. A piercing stare burned into the back of his skull like the light of the yellow sun. Remaining suspended from the wooden beam, he scanned the room twice over. The ambient sounds of blood - seeping into the wood and dripping down into the room below - was ever constant. Victor's body ached as he battled with the desire to drop to his knees and give into the hunger. His body craved nourishment, but his mind was sharp to the task at hand. He had been sent to the mortal plane by his father and - while his father would greatly approve of such violence - murdering everything in their path would only draw attention and slow them down.

Releasing his grip on the beam, Victor dropped to the ground. He twisted and twirled in the air like a weightless feather, and his open shirt writhed behind him moments before he landed on his feet. A heap of intestine squirted out from beneath his black boots.

"Did you do this?" Victor questioned softly as he buttoned up his shirt.

The presence of his sister was strong. He could feel her stepping out from the shadows behind him. She was completely silent. Turning to face her, Victor cut through the darkness with a sharp stare. Spotting the sibling, his gaze was a fine blade pressed to flesh, but the girl was unscathed by his judgement; rather, she reveled in it.

Lilith was standing in the darkest corner of the room. Her hair was soaked in blood and her face was painted red. "I was hungry ... and bored," she said with a twisted smile. "But mostly bored," she added, looking on to the collection of gore that was strewn about the room.

"Why did you bring them up here?" Victor complained as he walked towards the bookshelf and picked up his belt.

He could hear his sword, Heart Cutter, whisper from beneath its sheathed home. The blade hungered for blood, and it could smell the feast that was strewn out about the room. Victor tried to ignore the whispers as he fastened the leather strap to his waist. He fiddled with the positioning of his father's bone fragment so that the heavy shard wouldn't dig into his side. He then reached behind the shelf and plucked his cloak from the window. The crimson pools of blood and gore stuck to the soles of his boots like creatures reaching up at him in hopes of salvation. He tried to ignore the sounds. He fastened the cape around his neck and made for the room's single entrance. He then wrapped the fingers of his right hand around the door's iron latch. The wood along the frame was splintered, and the lock was now rendered useless.

"I didn't," the sister smirked. "These were," she paused, "just the ones that ran upstairs." She dropped to the ground and pressed her hands into a pool of warm blood. Victor could hear her giggle as she toyed with the juices like a child playing with its meal.

Victor paused with his hand still wrapped around the door's latch. The bloodbath was strong on his senses, but what lie beyond the door was far more overpowering. He took a deep breath and closed his eyes for a moment as he fought off the feral urge to feast.

"Isn't *God* supposed to offer protection from monsters like us?" The sister cackled, "As per usual, the old bigot is nowhere to be found. Floating on a cloud with one of his many mistresses I'm sure."

Victor ignored the comment. He opened his eyes and tugged on the door's latch. To no surprise, the scent of carnage washed over him like the waves of saline waters crashing into a small, single-sailed sloop. His spine tingled as he again closed his eyes. His father's whispers tugged at his core and he wanted nothing more than to give in to this temptation. Opening his eyes once more, he spotted a mass of mangled bodies resting at the base of the wooden stairwell - a heap of meat and bone blended together like mush and resting at the heart of the pile was one of his sister's prized kills.

Victor descended the stairs. The barmaid, Joanna, was lying still within the heap of gore, and her hands were stretched forward

- resting along the wooden stairs. She had bled out trying to climb up to the second floor. Her backside was littered with an assortment of lesions that were deep enough to expose bone. Her pretty face was perfectly still, and her chin rested against the fourth step. Her blonde hair was torn, and a bald patch of blotched skin oozed blood from the crown of her head. The girl's eyes were open and lifeless. Her warm expression had gone cold and her green stare was out of focus.

It pained Victor to see such a kind soul fall victim to the torment of his family. Guilt was a stress that was heavy like stone. It was one of his father's favorite weapons. Victor rose into the air and glided over the woman's mangled body. Careful to not disturb her eternal slumber, he only planted his feet back against the ground's surface when he was clear of the body below. He stepped out into the open bar area. Bodies were strewn about from wall to wall. Most of the corpses were merely scraps. Victor's sister had only left the barmaid intact, likely to toy with her brother's emotions - or lack thereof.

Victor parted the sea of blood and walked towards the bar's exit. Intestines hung from the ceiling like meat left to smoke, and the bodies below were twisted and mangled in such a way as to confirm his sister's boredom. Most men were deserving of such violence. The notion of good and evil was something that Victor was raised to despise. All of the men of the mortal plane were evil. All of the angels in the heavens were liars, and all of the demons across the nine hells were deceitful.

Victor turned back to face the barmaid. One of her feet was twisted and a broken shard of bone poked out from beneath her soft skin.

This reality lacked truth or morals, but- sometimes- an effulgent gem of hope glistened through this hour of despair. Such a thing was only a prize in the eyes of his father, and his sister revealed in the pleasures of annihilation.

Victor approached the bar's exit. His sister appeared from the shadows and levitated behind him.

"Go on and feast, little brother," she whispered into his ear.

Victor placed a hand on the exit latch and paused for a moment as he entertained the thought. In a volley of sporadic thoughts, he imagined himself rolling around on the floor. He pictured himself bathing in the bloodbath and feasting on the remains of the fresh kill. The gluttonous thoughts were blissfully delightful. He pulled at the exit's latch. The iron groaned and the door cried out as it drifted open at the hands of a cool wind beyond the tavern.

Victor's eyes sharpened as he exchanged stares with a woman standing on the opposing side of the now-open door. With frayed hair and a broken face, the barmaid gazed back at the vampire with her soft, green eyes. She silently plead for mercy in this hour of despair.

Victor's upper lip flared as a burst of anger coursed through his veins.

"Don't you want me?" Joanna questioned. Her lips were seductive and, despite the lesions across her bruised skin, she still wore a softness that was not of this world.

"Get out of my fucking head," Victor growled, and the woman lifted her chin to the sky to cackle. With each burst of laughter, the pitch in her tone grew more distorted.

"Let's stop with all of the games," the woman said at last as she ran her hands up along her broken chest. Wounds further stretched and tore with her motions, and the lacerations grew deeper as blood leaked from the lesions like a fall after a midsummer storm. "I know you want me," she beckoned through the soft-yet-seductive tone. "I can tell by the way that you look at me."

Victor seethed beneath his skin. He tightly clenched his jaw and cut deep into his gums. "Get out of my way," he said with a sense of tension that bleed from his vocal chords.

The woman lifted a hand to her tattered clothes. She tugged at the cloth. The strip of fabric was quick to tear away, and she discarded it to the floor like the fine lace of a sexual gown. With her breasts exposed, she arched her back and leaned forward. She then latched on to Victor's belt with one hand and caressed his manhood with another.

Victor extended a palm and pushed the girl away. She made a seductive groan as she stumbled backward and burst into shadow. Victor looked to his hand. It was covered in blood.

Lifting his eyes back towards the horizon, he savored in the sight of the peaceful landscape. Beyond the lingering smoke was a line of pine trees. They swayed under the fresh winds that blew in from the east and washed over the spiny limbs like cleansing waters. Victor inhaled a breath of the crisp air. It stung his lungs. The pain was uniquely satisfying. He stepped out into the night and made his way towards the back of the saloon where he had left Midnight under the shelter of a stable.

The team of horses stood in silence. Although they were all fully grown, they appeared to be ponies when standing beside Midnight. Victor approached the horses. He unfastened them, one by one, from their posts and then smacked them on the arses. They neighed before taking off into the night. Only Midnight remained.

Lilith appeared beside her brother. She was still disguised as Joanna. "How about a hunt?" She offered as she watched the horses run out across the field.

"No," Victor said sternly. "The daylight has already set us back."

"It will only take a minute," she added, leaning forward and preparing to give chase.

Victor lifted his hand and threw it across his sister's bleeding chest. His open palm smacked her skin and she flinched.

"I *said* no."

Lilith smirked and then leaned inward so that her bare breast would slide across her brother's open palm. Victor withdrew his hand and unfastened the great steed from its wooden post. He then ran his fingers through the stallion's mane.

"You like them?" Lilith questioned, dropping her disguise and taking on her usual form. The blood remained, and her clothes were stained.

Victor ignored her as he continued to stroke the charger's

mane. Unlike the rest of the coarse fur that covered the beast's body, its mane was silky and soft to the touch. He listened to the ambient noises of the night before gliding up and onto the steed. The horse snorted and Victor dug his heels into the beast, which triggered its inner burst of power and speed. The two took off into the night. If they made haste, they'd reach the walls of Astra' Kandra in two day's travel.

Part Five
The Second Dawn

Victor and Midnight rode far into the eventide. At some point in their ride, Lilith had appeared and taken a seat on the saddle behind her brother. Her face was covered in dry coagulated blood, and the crimson smelled of animal. At some point between the bloodbath back at the White Stag and returning to her brother's side, Lilith had found and murdered an animal. She was strangely quiet as they ventured further down empty roads and across barren plains.

"The sun will be coming up soon," Lilith broke her silence. "We'd better find somewhere to take shelter for the day."

Hills rolled into one another at the heart of the distant horizon. The landscape beyond was beginning to glow. The two had followed an eastward path along a tree line and they hadn't seen other travelers or a town since leaving the White Stag. It would take them hours to cross the grassy plain ahead, and even then, Victor was unsure as to what may lie beyond the rolling hills.

"God can be clever sometimes," Lilith asserted as the two arrived at the same conclusion.

Venturing across the open field at this hour would lead to their untimely demise. Victor tugged at the charger's reins and Midnight slowed along the tree line.

We'll have to cut into the forest until nightfall, Victor thought as the charger came to a stop and he glided down from atop the steed.

The forest was overly dense and eerily quiet. He tugged at the reins as he walked forward, guiding the horse closely behind him. Lilith remained seated on the saddle and Victor caught a glimpse of her expression as she sat in silence. She wore the rare look of concern, but Victor disregarded the thought. Just as soon as he broke through the tree line, Midnight let out a sharp neigh and lifted his front legs into the air. The reins slipped from Victor's grasp, and the charger twirled freely. Lilith was thrown from the steed. A loud crack cut through the early morning air and she squealed in pain as Victor dove for the reins. He grabbed hold of the leather straps and fought to maintain control. Calling out to the horse through silent, mental whispers, he worked to regain control over the spooked charger and ease its frightened mind.

Lilith stood to her feet. Her arm was twisted and broken. Jagged, white bone stuck out from her forearm. She rolled her eyes and hissed as she pressed the palm of her hand against the cartilage.

With his hands on the reins, Victor turned back to inspect the tree line. He was greeted with total silence. There were no birds or bugs, critters or wind. The leaves were still, and the greenery was dense. A soft glow captured Victor's attention. He knelt to the ground and brushed away some twigs and debris to unearth a glowing rune etched into stone.

"A ward," Lilith hissed as she slid the broken cartilage back beneath her ruptured skin. She closed her eyes and wailed for a moment at the esoteric pulsations of fresh internal wounds.

The stone was glowing a soft green. The symbols etched

into the rock were in a strange cursive that Victor couldn't decipher.

"No doubt the elves of the forest are to blame for such a thing," Lilith snickered. "They are loyal to the druidic circles, and their magic runs writhe through this forest." She inched a little closer to her brother, cradling her broken arm as she lingered. "It's a noxious scent. I'm surprised you couldn't smell it."

The air did smell different. It was fresh and heavy with the scent of healthy plants and wildlife, but Victor had never encountered druids or elves before. He had only ever known of them through stories told across the nine hells. Their kind, though seen as sinners in the eyes of the creator, were abstained from damnation, and- as such- never plunged into the rings of hell.

Victor pressed a pair of fingers against the glowing rune. Nothing happened. He had been naive to the lingering fragrance of foreign magics. It was disguised well amidst the scent of fresh air and woods.

"These glyphs of warding are not scribed into stone to keep us away, little brother."

Victor lifted his eyes to the forest beyond the blessing.

"These traps are for mortal men," Lilith added.

The forest was thick and overgrown with green leaves, vines, and shrubs. Full of vitality, the trees leached nutrients from the soil and passed their gift of life onto the creatures of the forest. There was silence beneath their veil of secrets.

"Either you endure the agony of the rising sun," Lilith gestured back towards the eastern horizon. Victor didn't bother turning to face the birthing dawn. The sun's rays were beginning to trickle up over the rolling hills, and it was only a matter of minutes before Victor would find himself subject to the burn of the scorching rays. "Or we make way through the forest." Lilith nodded back towards the line of trees and shrubs. The overgrown trees offered shelter from the sun, and the plant life beneath the branches only further worked to spread distorted pockets of total darkness.

Victor rose to his feet and tugged at Midnight's reins. The

horse was fearful of the forest, but it ultimately gave in to its master's commands. It trailed behind the vampire, and the two of them stepped forward through the line of trees. Victor felt unscathed for breaching the magically-defined barrier. It was as his sister had said. The warding runes were not in place for him. These lands belonged to the druids, and the war between elves and men rivaled only the bloodbath between heaven and hell. Perhaps it was because of this that Satan felt neither admiration nor distaste for the elves. They were a mysterious race who excelled in the art of murder. Often silent and always dexterous, the elves were natural born killers, and men were merely swine for slaughter compared to these champions of the forest.

Victor could feel the presence of wildlife lingering in the shadows. Critters retreated further into the darkness as the vampire pressed deeper into the thicket. A haze of fog rose up from the earth and obscured any sort of view forward. Turning back to face the outer tree line, Victor watched as the sun's rising rays were devoured by the thick wall of plant life. He wouldn't be able to keep his bearings for long, so he decided that he shouldn't venture too deep. He tied Midnight's reins around the basin of a thick wood and then took to a larger ancient tree. He scaled up against the side of the bark and broke through the veil of the eerie fog.

Birds chirped above the veil and leaves blustered under a cool wind. The sounds of the forest had been encased behind the magical barrier, and only now that Victor was within the thicket could he hear the many accents of wildlife.

Victor floated back down from the oak and sliced through the fog. He returned to the ground. A trio of soft pops could be heard beneath his boots. Before Victor had time to think, he was digested in a cloud of shimmering blue spores. He had mistakenly landed on a bed of fungi. Small bulbs were splitting and tearing open beneath his feet.

Victor lunged forward, trying not to inhale any of the microorganisms. Hell had hallucinogenic fungi: Bahl fungi was grown in the belly of a great demon and, when ingested, the user would trip through spacetime and loose themselves for upwards of a thousand years. Victor was unsure of what secrets the spores of the mortal plane carried, but he couldn't risk finding out. Carelessly lifting himself up into the air, he quickly sliced through the fog and collided with a thick branch before plunging back down to the earth. He was again encased in a cloud of spores. He had landed on his backside, and directly on a second bed of mushrooms. The breath had been leached from his lungs, and he was left wheezing on the ground. The spores rained down upon him like fireflies twinkling in the twilight.

Victor sprung to his feet and pressed his eyes forward. The spores continued to fall beneath his waistline. The world around him was quick to melt and sway.

Essco litaar-mass, the wind called.

"Lilith," Victor softly growled.

He had lost sight of his sister soon after entering the thicket, and he hoped that perhaps she was playing tricks on him. He had left Midnight tied to one of the smaller trees, but so too was the charger gone. The vampire slowly turned around and noticed that the landscape had changed. The thick forest floor was now mostly clear of debris, and a sea of green ferns swayed under the veil of towering trees for as far as the eye could see. The way back to the open plain was no longer near, and Victor found himself standing in the center of an endless forest.

Essco-litaar-mass...

Victor rested the palm of his hand against his sheathed blade. Heart Cutter called out to him with a desire for blood, but Victor ignored the pleading cries of the lingering spirit that was trapped within steel so that he could continue to scan through the open thicket.

Essco-litaar-mass...

The gentle wind spoke in a strangely seductive tone. It beckoned Victor forward. The vampire cautiously made his way through the eerie forest. He'd turn back from time to time to find that the landscape would shift again and again. His bearings were truly gone. It reminded him of the tricks that Death would play.

There were no plants or wildlife in purgatory, but this forest played games in a similar manner.

Movement from behind a trio of trees captured Victor's attention. He caught the silhouette of someone taking shelter behind one of the ancient timbers. The vampire was quick to lift up off the ground and glide forward with his hand still resting against the hilt of his weapon. He reached the place of hiding only to discover nothing but ruffling ferns and a lingering wind. He lifted his eyes and scanned through the forest. A muddy handprint was smudged along the tree's outer shell. Victor ran a finger across the stain. The soil was still wet.

Whispers, spoken in an ancient tongue, called out through the forest and Victor remained idle as he listened to their cry.

Elves, he thought. *Their trickery is uncanny.*

Just then, the creaking sound of a timber's sway cracked through the air and Victor found himself suspended in the air by the heels of his boots. It all happened as quick as lightning. The limbs of a tree had lashed out and snared the vampire. The tight squeeze on his ankles was tough and true. He didn't bother fighting against the restraints and instead dangled freely, suspended in the air.

"You come to this sacred forest with aspirations of defile ... oh, dear sweet child..." an unseen entity called from the shadows of the woodland. The voice was soft yet sharp - its presence both soothing and of mysterious importance. The dialect was common, but the accent was strong like molasses sticking to the surface of the mouth to which the words were muttered.

Victor remained wordless as he swung freely from the tree. A distorted fog crept in towards the vampire. It encased him in twilight and left the woodlands unseen to his naked eye.

"You are but a child," the voice called, whispering closely from Victor's left-hand side before drifting over towards the right. "A child of grave importance, the son of Satan, walks freely through the domain of the ancient forest?" The voice grew angry and the words cut deeply into the Vampire's pale skin.

Victor grit his teeth as lesions tore open across his face.

The wall of fog receded and left on the ground was the broken body of a brown rabbit. The still corpse was mangled badly and crimson cuts ran deeply beneath its tattered fur. Victor could only assume that the cuts on his face mimicked faintly some of the rabbit's scars.

There was innocence in wildlife - a purity and balance that tugged at Victor's heartless chest. Despite the physical attack on his body, he was left feeling pity for the dead critter.

"The children of my domain are off limits to both the angels of heaven *and* the demons of hell," the fog cried before bleeding forth and encasing the vampire once more.

Victor was left hissing and twitching in pain as cuts continued to open up across the surface of his skin.

The fog receded and, left towering behind the broken rabbit, was the speaker in its true and horrific form. The monstrous humanoid figure birthed plants from its tough, bark-like skin. Green sprouts and moss covered most of its body like clothing. The great antlers of a stag hung from atop its head. Its twisted face reflected sorrow by way of black, inky stains beneath its cold, dead eyes. The bark creaked as the figure spoke.

"We have given too much to be betrayed!" The creature bellowed.

Victor came to understand the monster for what it was. It was said that dryads, a native children of the forest, bridged the connection between druidic circles and elves.

Many a curious eyes could be seen peeking out from the pockets of darkness that swirled beyond the dryad. Slanted and feminine, the watchers were silent and many. Victor could only assume that the observers were the forest elves, the mysterious race of human-like creatures who lived in the wilds and strayed far away from the likes of man.

Branches lashed out from shadows towards Victor. The child of Satan was branded again and again by the fall of earthen whips.

Druidic magic was strangely foreign to Victor. It was beyond the grasp of both heaven and hell. It worked closely with Death at times, but was never servant or aligned with any singular pantheon or entity. Rather, the druidic domains were circles of magic that worked outside of the laws of reality. God had come to believe that these circles worshiped Satan, but it simply wasn't true. Their allegiance was their own. Through the misinformation that God had been fed, Satan had grown fond of the mysterious circles and- as such- a pact was made long ago.

Victor endured the stinging pain out of a nagging curiosity and listened to the dryad as it continued to speak.

"Your father is without allegiance to our domain. He has taken something of great importance to us in a deal that many believe to be lopsided and unfair."

The deal that the creature referred to was in regards to one of Satan's first lovers. In exchange for the soul of a moon goddess, Satan and his legion of tormentors would leave nature as it is. Victor's father was surprisingly true to his word, at least when it came to blood pacts. Satan's followers had been led to believe that it was lust between the two differing parties that had driven them to be together, while the druidic folk had seen it for what -perhaps - it really was: a great sacrifice made - unwillingly by the goddess - in order to ensure the safety of her people. To this day, the allfather keeps the mistress locked behind the walls of a stone prison. It is said that he visits her from time to time and he has impregnated this moon many times over. Each of these encounters has resulted in the birthing of a grotesque, stillborn child.

"And you wish for me to change that?" Victor scoffed, still suspended in the air. He wore the branding of fresh wounds across his face.

"No child has voice enough to overthrow his father," the dryad corrected. "I demand that you stay out of our forests. If you walk the mortal plane, then you do so without bringing harm to our dominion."

Victor had no such desire to bring harm to the creatures of the woodland, and the offer was easy to accept. He had been sent to the mortal plane by his father, and he only walked these lands with a singular purpose at heart. Despite these truths, he indulged himself a little further in the pleasures of both pain and conferring.

"Where is my sister?" Victor called from above.

The inky black marks across the dryad's twisted face shifted and altered the creature's expression into that of inquiry. It was as if to ask without words whether the child was true to kinship.

"The firstborn is lost amidst our borders," the dryad was slow to answer.

Victor wondered if the creature had referred to Lilith by that name because she were older than he, or because she was once the first woman to be created by God. She was originally made of the same dirt as Adam and destined to be the wife of the first man, but the soil that had birthed her had been tainted by Satan. Lilith had refused to be servant to a man and she left the Garden of Eden soon after reaching sexual maturity. She had lived a long and fruitful life with sexual misandry and murder at the center of desire before succumbing to a poppy overdose and plunging into hell to stand alongside her true father for all eternity.

"Never would a miscreant to our domain be welcome in such a sacred forest," the dryad finished.

It was this form of discernment that had sparked the extensive war between elves and men long ago. The men of the mortal plane knew little of the druids and elves. They had come to believe the lie that God had created wildlife for man's consumption and nourishment. Victor wasn't sure of the druid's true origins, but he knew that the druidic circles of the mortal plane had staked claim over the fate of such creatures. It was a curious matter, and Victor contemplated it further as he swayed from the tree, the cool winds stinging at the open lacerations across his face.

"I am merely seeking shelter from the sun and its storm of scorching rays. I wish to bring no harm to the children of the forest," Victor finally obliged.

"But you *are* marked, sweet child," the dryad cried. "Death follows you like a curse, and the reaper's hunger is insoluble."

The dryad exhaled a breath of thick fog into the twilight air. Victor watched as his vision was barred, and then he felt the tight grip around his ankles vanish. The trees had let go of Victor and he was now plunging quickly through the fog. He twirled in the air and tried to levitate safely down, but gravity pulled him against his will. His bearings were soon lost as he continued to fall for seconds that became minutes. He ultimately landed, headfirst, into the stinging cold earth. The sounds of cracking bones echoed across the ground of an empty forest. Trying to stand, he grunted and rolled, but only collapsed back down into the earth. Writhe with agony and pain, the vampire froze at the sound of a familiar voice.

"You've played their games, sweet brother."

Victor lifted his eyes to find his sister standing beside the basin of a dead, leafless tree.

"And it has only brought you pain," she added. Kneeling to her brother and caressing his wounded face.

The night had come again, and the two siblings found themselves abandoned along the outer edge of the forest. Victor's steed had been left tied to a tree beside his sister. Both of the children exited the forest and Victor never told his sister of the dryad and the lashings - in that the affliction was punishment for her doings.

Part Six
A War Between Men

Victor and Lilith exited the forest under the cover of twilight, for the new moon had risen and the sun had set at some point during Victor's tumble back down towards Earth.

"What would Mother say if she saw her beautiful boy like this?" Lilith cried in regards to Victor's wounds. They were healing all too slowly. "His soft skin torn to shreds like the fine linens of an expensive whore."

"Mother *was* a whore," Victor argued, taking advantage of the opportunity to shift the topic of conversation. His tone was raspy and coarse.

Lilith's eyes dilated as shock and anger mingled in the depths of her belly.

"Mother was a *succubus,* and one of the most sought-after prizes in all the nine hells!"

Victor scowled and continued walking until Midnight was

clear of the trees and forest. He cared not for such stories. The mother that Lilith spoke of was the queen of lust. She hadn't birthed Lilith, but Victor's sister still spoke highly of the demonic wench nonetheless.

"They say that Mother enjoyed altering her form, but she mostly looked like me. Her black hair was long and soft like silk. Her skin was smooth and warm like innards. She enjoyed both sexual conquest and temptation." Lilith's voice trailed off as she went on with a description that was only tale, and Victor began to tune her out as he climbed up onto Midnight, securing the reins tightly within his grip. "She had the tightest, most succulent flower of any woman who came before her," Lilith continued ranting. "Or at least she did," she paused and Victor knew of what came next. "Before *you* tore it to pieces... *Fucking* savage."

Victor's face remained stone. The volley of words slapped at his broken skin like holy water, but he merely gazed forward in a lifeless stare as Midnight began to walk him down the isle of redemption. His father had always hated him, but Victor was an asset to sin and, as such, Satan was keen to keep the son close.

"Nobody knows where she is now," Lilith inserted, gliding up to take a seat behind her brother. Victor could feel her expression grow soft. "She knew that Father would never want her again. Some say she walks the mortal plane, seducing and straddling men like swine. I pray it isn't true."

You pray, Victor silently mocked. Lilith always did have a way with words.

The exchange between brother and sister stopped there. The two remained silent in their journey eastward. They crossed through the field and climbed over many hills before the grassy terrain turned to grey rock and barren wasteland. The scent of murder wafted in the air. Carried on the wings of a crisp, nightward air, the smell was of fresh kill and warm corpses. Lilith shifted in the saddle and Victor's stomach growled as he was ever reminded of his famished hunger. Even Heart Cutter began to stir. Trapped within its sheathe, the blade called out to its master, for it yearned to taste the fresh kills.

Coming to the alpine peak of a rocky terrain, the earth had opened up to reveal a wasteland of conquest and war. Many mortal factions of men collided in the distance. Thousands of torches, coupled with the moon's shine, served to brighten the battlefield for all the world to see.

Victor halted Midnight and watched from atop the steed as two opposing lines collided. The soft cries of butchery and murder, bloodshed and carnage drifted through the nighttide air. Lilith dismounted and crept closer to the rocky ledge. Men fell at the hands of their distant cousin. Catapults launched balls of flame into opposing sides and flaming arrows followed suit.

"If there is one thing that can be said about men, it's that they make for great cannon fodder to Father's ranks," Lilith snickered. "These *sinners* will be useful in the great war to come."

She wasn't wrong. Very rarely did mortal souls make it deep into the nine rings of hell. They were the weakest of Satan's forces, but they dwarfed any other faction in terms of sheer numbers and they were always easy to control.

"Let's go," Victor commanded from atop his steed.

Lilith turned back to face her brother. She rolled her eyes like a disaffectionate teenager, rebellious to authority. She cupped her broken arm. Victor was sure that- had she not been crippled- she'd perhaps venture down into the gully and toy with the warring factions. She levitated back up onto the saddle and took her seat with her legs hanging from Midnight's right. She was facing the carnage below, and her attention was fully submerged in the murky waters of bloodshed.

The two siblings continued along the path. The dying squeals of men- facing the end of it all- beseeched their minds and pled against their hunger as they traveled. If only mortals knew of what came next. What lies beyond Death's cold escort was either an existence alongside God or, more often than not, a life of servitude to the great beast below the earth. One was either a servant or a slave, and resting along the tip of a molten skewer for all of eternity didn't seem half bad in the greater scheme of things. For living in sin only leads to becoming a part of it all. One singular cesspool of darkness: a stinking rot fused into the skin of hatred and agony. Forever and ever with their feet pressed to the flames of the abyss, the damnable would be slave to beast in ways that knew not of limits or injustice. Victor was almost jealous of such a fate. To have a say in the matter. He'd never truly know.

"We should probably get off the main road," Lilith suggested a few minutes into their continued travel.

Victor rejected the offer and stayed true to the path. He could only assume that the woodlands to the north fell under druidic protection. Regardless of whether it were true or not, the dryad had made it quite clear that neither Victor nor his sister were welcome in the forest.

Lilith sighed. "They *will* challenge us."

Victor glanced ahead. The trail that wrapped around the edge of the rocky terrain was outlined in forest. A line of tents, horses, torches, and red banners rested along the far end of the rim. With no choice but to ride forward, the two siblings continued onwards towards the encampment.

"Halt, in the name of the king!" A voice barked from ahead after Victor had come within eyesight of the camp's dwellers.

"Blech," Lilith guffawed. "Men are so eager to serve. They bow to kings for, they are promised significance in a world without meaning. The twilight is endless and they are but specs in the boundless ocean: significant to none."

Victor and Lilith continued to ride forward. The man was a knight, and as the siblings furthered their approach, the soldier was accompanied by a second. They were a pair now of fully plated warriors with their hands resting along the hilt of fine broadswords blades. The two soldiers were ready to draw and defend the encampment should the siblings advance in their approach. They were clad in silver armor from head to toe. A red cross was painted athwart their plated chest pieces.

"They revel in sin but fear only Death," Lilith spoke unheedingly. "They wear tribute to God, but tell me, Brother, who do they *really* serve?"

Lilith's arm was still broken badly. The injury would require another day of healing before she could make use of the ligament again. Sapped of her energy and focus, she was unable to wear her disguise of transparency. Victor tightened his grips on the leather straps and dug his heels deeper into Midnight's muscular belly. The horse ignited in a burst of speed and trampled through the guards with ease. Victor could hear the sound of his sister giggling as the men grunted and wailed. Their armor was rendered useless under the weight of trampling hooves.

Soldiers bled out from the nearby tents and Victor responded with the unsheathing of his own blade. As the warriors sprung towards the siblings and their steed, Victor cast Heart Cutter to the sky and the weapon, a slave to its desire for blood, flew through the air and pierced cleanly into the chest of a nearby knight. The man screamed as the weapon tore cleanly his ribcage. He dropped to the ground, but not before the weapon continued to soar into the heart of a second soldier.

Victor and Lilith had cleared past the encampment and the son lifted his hand into the air to call his weapon back. It did not come. He turned his head and found that his sister was giggling with joy as she watched the onslaught. Victor tugged on the reigns and slowed Midnight to a steady gallop. He spun the horse around and watched as Heart Cutter deflected blows and dropped the clad knights one by one. Victor twitched his upper lip and closed his eyes. Calling out to the blade, he imposed his will and forced the spirit weapon to return. He opened his eyes to find the weapon resting in the palm of his open hand. He closed his fist and lowered the sword. It was dripping with warm blood. He wiped the blade clean against his pant leg before returning the weapon back into its sheath. It cried out in anger and despair, for its pleasure had been cut short amidst climax.

Victor looked at Lilith. She slowly shook her head and tried to combat an impeding smile. The weapon never failed to impress her. Victor returned his gaze forward and unleashed Midnight's strength in speed. The charger bolted forward into the night and the siblings left the bleeding bodies to lie still beneath the twinkling stars in the sky.

After an hour's travel east, Victor and Lilith came to the outskirts of a small town. An old wooden sign read *Motious Sinclair.* The city streets were barren, and little light shone within the impoverished homes.

"With war so close to their doorstep, the town's men have been called to the frontlines," Lilith assumed out loud.

Exerted, Midnight had grown fatigued and the steed began to minutely sway. Victor dropped their speed to a slow tread. He closed his eyes and pressed way into the steed's mind. Through the beast's exhaustion, the charger's mind was swollen with a web of conflicting thoughts: worry, fright, depravity, confusion. Victor tried to ease the mental wounds. He felt sympathy for the beast, and he was at fault for pushing it so hard through the night, but they couldn't stop in this town. They had to reach Astra' Kandra by sunrise.

The siblings rode through the town's barren streets. Victor rubbed Midnight's mane with one hand and watched through the darkness for any movement. He could feel eyes unseen pressing against his skull. They were being watched, but by who and from where, Victor was unsure.

"Ain't she a pretty one," a man reflected out loud, breaking the silence in the air. He stepped forth from the shadows of a nearby ally and walked alongside the siblings and their steed.

"Yeah she is." A second man appeared.

Victor maintained his gaze forward and refused to even so much as look at the men.

A quarter-dozen riders came forth from ahead. The horsemen were men. Wormish and unclean, they were scoundrels, drifters, and pirates: the type of men who float from town to town in search of things that are not theirs. Gold, women, and ale were the best of prizes to be claimed in the eyes of these monsters.

"Might we have a taste?" One of the men pleaded as he reached for Lilith's skirt.

Victor wasn't afraid of them. He had fought in many of the wars below and killing men of the mortal plane was child's play. Most of the men below were obedient servants to Satan. Their will had been broken long ago, and they kneeled before their king so that their suffrage in eternity may be minimal. He had to get Lilith away from them before she could do something reckless.

"Hold on," Victor muttered to his sister before tapping into Midnight's strength.

Although exhausted, the loyal steed obeyed and pushed forward through the town. This only served to excite the pirates and a game of cat and mouse ensued.

Another quarter-dozen riders bled forth from the ransacked town. They whooped and hollered obscenities and cries of excitement as they rode down the siblings like wolves in chase of prey.

"We can't outride them," Lilith cackled, taking note of Midnight's newfound weakness. "Perhaps it's our turn to have a little fun."

Victor wouldn't have it. They were close now to Astra' Kandra, and Midnight only needed to push a little further in order to outright ditch the scoundrels.

Approaching a small stone bridge, the siblings crossed over running water and then Victor's mind went white.

A bit of time passed before Victor came to.

"Victor!" The sister cried. "Get up, Victor!"

The vampire was lying on the ground beneath a clear night sky. His sister was calling for him, but the sound was lost to a stinging white noise that cut clear through his mind.

Victor shakily forced himself to his feet. He caught a glimpse of Midnight. The horse was twirling and screaming in the dirt across the way. It had crossed the bridge but had also been thrown to the ground when both Lilith and Victor were dismounted. It's front left leg was snapped and twisted badly. It cried in agony as it struggled to stand.

Victor turned to face his sister's call. She too was climbing to her feet.

"The fucking bastard!" She cried, choking up a mouthful of blood. "He has empowered the water so that we cannot cross!"

It seemed that God had bolstered another defense for his

children. The siblings were barred from crossing living, running water.

The ringing in Victor's skull continued as he watched his sister collapse back into the dirt. His eyes went out of focus and he caught sight of the scoundrels who were chasing after them. They drew near, and Midnight's blood-curdling screams only added further to the burden of confusion and doubt that rested upon Victor's broad shoulders.

"Seems they took a tumble," one of the men chuckled as he came to a stop before Lilith.

Eight more men came to rest alongside the first. Victor could smell the iron coursing through their veins. They were excited, and their heart rates were elevated. Through the static and confusion, Victor could hear the calls of their beating hearts. He stepped towards his sister and ignored the hoots and hollers being stricken down on him. His mind had fragmented and he had gone feral. The only thought, a mere smudge of emotion to be had, was that of blood.

In a flash of ebony and red, he streaked across the sky and dismounted one of the men. Victor's thirst was unquenchable, his will infallible, and so he sunk his teeth into the man's neck and leeched. The blood was succulent and warm. This was, perhaps, his greatest desire. It had been tugging at his heartless chest for some time, and now, only through a feral bloodlust, did he tap into his own strength and drain the man of all life.

The other riders looked on in horror as Victor continued to feast. They withdrew weapons: blunted steel with jagged edges. Letting go of his prize was as difficult a task as any, but there were more banquets to attend. He blinked from horse to horse and dismounted the men one by one. Using his nails, he cut deeply into their faces. The scoundrels fought back with a sense of dexterity and speed. They were ruthless and strong but crippled with fear. They died all the same. Stuttering and crying, weeping and moaning. Their flesh was delicate and their blood was surprisingly exquisite.

Victor's feral rage was soothed by the fullness instilled by drinking plenty. His cup had overrunneth, and his focus returned to the present. Some of the men, though gravely wounded, were still alive. Victor stood to his feet and looked for sister. She was stringing one of the men up into a nearby tree. She had strangled the man with his own entrails, and she was now laughing maniacally at his struggle for survival. It was a useless attempt. His belly had been torn open and his innards seeped out. He died before she could manage to hang him, but she went on with hoisting him up by his intestine anyway.

The desperate cries were many. The survivors were bleeding out on the ground. Their skin had been shredded at Victor's hand, and many of them harbored puncture wounds instilled by his teeth. Heart Cutter wanted in on the bloodbath, but Victor ignored the blade's call. He met with the survivors and, careful not to drain them of too much, he devoured their will and left them in the dirt to turn. They wiggled and wormed as they shrieked in agony at a transformation that the world had never once seen before. Their bones ruptured through their fingertips, and they grew claws in place of the balls of their fingers. Their jaws twisted and warped and they grew fangs from their face. They'd never be able to fully close their mouths again, but that was the least of these men's concerns.

Lilith returned to her brother's side. She lifted a brow as she watched the men scream and twirl in the dirt. Their backs cracked and their chests rose as the transformation continued.

"What have you done?" Lilith questioned with intriguement.

"They belong to me now," Victor said coldly as he continued to watch the six men claw at the dirt in agony. He then glanced back across the stream where Midnight lie still on the ground. The steed had died a painfully horrific death. Internal bleeding and a broken leg. Even worse, it had been left to suffer alone right up until it drew its final breath. Victor couldn't see him, but he sensed Death's presence. He was a particularly cruel entity, and Victor wanted to lash out at the reaper for taking the steed. In truth, it was Victor's own ignorance that had led to the untimely death of his horse. He hated himself for it, but he tried to bury the thought, as it came with a sense of emotion he'd rather not believe he had.

Victor looked at his sister. She was still watching the men in the dirt and trying to understand what was happening to them. The men would be blindly obedient to Victor once the transformation was fully complete. He had not only consumed their vitality, but he had also drained them of their will. Only hollow shells, servants of Death on loan to the son would remain.

"How?" Lilith pressed. She and Victor could turn many, but only through whispers and pacts: dark deals and temptation. Even then, turning someone into a follower was never as cut and dry as simply sinking your teeth into their skin and leeching.

"They follow me... for now," Victor began as he watched one of the men squirm and writhe within the dirt. "But they are on loan, and I don't know what will happen to them after I fall."

"On loan?" Lilith squinted as she thought on the comment for a moment. "Oh, dear brother," she snickered, piecing the puzzle together. "Father *would* be proud."

"Come now," Victor said softly, making way for one of the scoundrel's abandoned steeds. "Dawn draws near, and the city should only lie just ahead."

Part Seven
The Third Dawn

Victor and Lilith rode their stolen steed around the stream. It brought them through a thinly wooded land that eventually led back around to the path towards Astra' Kandra. They rode for an hour before their new charger grew weak. It was malnourished and lacked the strength that Midnight had once harbored. The two dismounted and continued on foot until a series of faint squeaks captured Victor's attention. It was coming from a nearby shrub and Victor froze as he listened to the cry.

Slowly, Victor approached the bush. He pulled back a wall of leaves to reveal a mischief of rats. They were mostly blind. They wavered their heads and twitched their noses as they tried to feel for something near.

"Rats," Lilith whispered coarsely. "Some of nature's great survivors. Their mischief is a tell: we are close to a city."

Victor knelt down and examined the rodents. Their fur was

greasy and they wobbled oddly as they darted one by one between the vampire's legs.

"Careful, brother," Lilith hissed. "Some of the more cynical druids of the wild have gifted them with plague. Chemical warfare."

Victor rose and turned to watch the rats wonder away. The lead rat scurried with a tilted head. Its movement was imbalanced. Its little pink nose was pressed to the ground and moving quickly as the rat was led purely by its sense of smell. Its eyes were open but glazed over and motionless. The animal was blind, and Victor felt something for the poor creature.

Ignoring his sister's heed, Victor took two steps towards the line of rats and knelt so that he could cup his hands around one of the greasy rodents. He picked up one of the rats and brought it to his face. He could hear his sister snicker. The rodent pressed its nose against Victor's skin. It could sense the rise in elevation and was careful to not leap blindly from Victor's hands.

Victor closed his eyes. He tried to bleed his thoughts into the rodent's mind, but there was a veil of fog that prevented the two minds from joining. The rat lifted its head. Its glossy eyes were grossly out of focus, but Victor knew that the creature was trying to look upon his face. Its mind was broken, and that meant that Victor could not speak unto it.

"Come, brother," Lilith said softly. "We are only minutes from the city gates."

Victor returned the rat to its mischief. The family of vermin embraced one another with the tips of their decrepit noses. Most of the brothers and cousins of the rat's clan were blind and with broken minds.

Lilith and Victor continued east along the road before they came upon the sound of unseen men. Creeping forward with caution, Victor discovered a trio of men standing idly in an open clearing. They had a wagon which was tied up to a pair of horses. A broken caravan lie beside them. Moss and rot had melded into the wood of the broken vehicle. The men lingered near their working caravan. They seemed to be bored and without purpose. Behind them was a vast wheat field that swayed from side to side before the gates of a great stone wall. Cream-colored buildings with brown trim and red roofing could be seen in the distance beyond the wall, and a golden steeple climbed higher than any other building in the landscape. Everything rested beneath the comfort of a crisp pink sky.

"Astra' Kandra," Lilith whispered as she shifted into her ethereal form for the first time in days.

Victor remained motionless under the canopy of shadows that the forest provided as he continued to fixate on the caravan of men. Unshaven and stinking of rum, sweat, and urine, the mortal men were scoundrels. One of them wore the sigil of Solomon around his neck.

Victor stepped out from the shadows and approached the three men. They barely paid him any mind as he approached. They spoke of women and their desires for sexual conquest and fine ale. It wasn't until Victor was standing directly before the grotesque men did they turn to properly face him.

"I help you?" One of the men slurred.

Victor's eyes crept from one subject to another. Each of the men shared the same ghoulish stare: a trademark of men destined to serve his Father. They were dressed in filthy rags and their stench was grossly unbearable.

Victor didn't need to answer, let alone say much of anything. The minds of these men were like jelly, and Victor silently spread the pectin on bread, for their will was easily shapeable to his.

"Been waitin' a while on you," one of the men complained as he pulled back a cloth tarp that hung draped across the backside of the wagon.

The scent of Death's noxious presence bled from out the open caravan. Wooden caskets were stacked in the back of the wagon. The third man climbed inside and worked to dislodge one of coffins from the pile. He passed it down to the other two men, who grunted and complained as they struggled to set it down on the ground. Hopping down from the caravan, the third man looked down to the coffin and then back up to Victor.

"Mr. Wellington. Duke Wellington," he read out loud the words that were etched across the wooden surface. "That's you," he added, gesturing towards Victor. He then withdrew a metal bar and violently slid the tool's end up under the sealed lid. Twisting and tugging, he pried the lid off to reveal the deceased corpse of a soldier whose eyes had been carved out from his skull. The man snickered at his two companions and they then emptied the coffin of its body. They dragged the corpse into the nearby brush and left it for the earth and the worms to feast upon. "There ye' have it. Hop on in," he instructed. "Ye' chariot awaits."

The sun was rising quickly and the line of light crept forward at a great, cleansing speed.

"Fuck the plan," Lilith pled, unbeknownst to the men. "You cannot trust these pigs!"

"No, I cannot," Victor said softly. He spoke in a tone that mortal minds could not hear. "Least of all, not after *you* butchered *their* king." His upper brow twitched as he fought back the sudden urge to go ballistic.

"The city priests will see through our deception. Even in my ethereal form, they will sense my presence," Lilith warned, glancing out towards the wall beyond.

"Well?" One of the men spat, growing impatient and unknowing of the conversation that Victor was having with his sister.

Victor glared at the man. He crept in through the scoundrel's iris and severed cleanly the basin of his brain stem. The man motionlessly dropped to the ground with a thud and his two companions gasped. They withdrew back towards the wagon and left Victor to his thoughts.

"I can draw them to the city gates," Lilith offered. "But not until nightfall."

Victor nodded as he stared down at the lifeless corpse.

"I will tell you this, oh sweet brother," Lilith's form shifted into the present and she ran her fingers across her brother's face. Victor remained unmoved as his sister caressed his skin. He could hear the other two men gasp as they watched the woman appear out of thin air. "You will need to tap into Father's rage if you wish to complete his task."

Victor had known of anger and rage, but he rarely ever let such a thing bleed from his pale skin. Born of the circle of lust, he was a creature of silence, deception, and desire. He preferred his methods of conquest, but he also knew that his sister was right in that God's chosen wouldn't be easily fooled. Their eyes could see through Satan's lies and, as such, Victor would be foolish to think that such a journey's end would be easy.

Lilith tugged at her brother's chin. She directed his stare into her ebony eyes and his vision sharpened as he looked into her.

"I'll see you back home," she said with a twinkle in her eyes before gently planting a kiss on her brother's lips.

Victor remained motionless. He watched as his sister's womanly form burst into shadow and she took to the canopy of nearby trees. With her gone, he looked back at the men, who stared blankly with faces of horror.

Victor said nothing as he glided down into the coffin. The men nailed the lid on and placed him into the back of the wagon as the light of the morning sun washed over the wooden sarcophagus.

Victor could feel the heat of the rising sun. He could see the light from between the fine cracks along the casket's walls, but as the cloth tarp was hung back up along the wagon's backside, so too was the sun again vanquished.

Victor heard the crack of a whip as one of the men called to the horses and the wagon began to rock. The son of Satan closed his eyes. It wouldn't take long for him to slip into the city, but he'd have to wait out the sun before he could rise from the casket and begin the endgame. He decided it best to sleep through the day to regain his strength and ensure that he was at full vitality before the witching hour of conquest and bloodshed befell the city.

It didn't take long for Victor to fall asleep within the coffin. He witnessed the deception of his nagging thoughts as they played for him a strange song of foreign emotion. A sequence of dreams overtook his conscious mind and he watched as Lilith walked up to the city portcullis. Men, outfitted in shining metal armor, inquired as to who she was. She offered a decrepit smile as she burst into shadow and bled through the steel bars of the portcullis. The darkness twirled into the standing presence of her physical form. She leapt through the air and shifted in and out of her ethereal form. Clawing at the eyes of mortal men and cutting through the armor of soldiers with utter ease, she murdered dozens within minutes which became hours throughout the eternal night. The bodies piled high all around her. It wasn't until she was fully surrounded by men in shining armor did she fall to a sea of metal and light.

The dream then shifted over to another point in spacetime, and Victor watched through his slumber as the shadow of his sister seeped through the cracks along the great stone wall. Civilians cried as she smirked from ear to ear and began her conquest of bloodshed anew. She littered the streets with bodies and viscera before priests dressed in white linens and golden bits of jewelry approached her with smirks and grins. They doused her in holy water and lashed out at her with wooden crosses. Lilith squealed in agony as her physical form was devoured at the hands of divine magic.

Victor's slumber then guided him over to a third and final vision. He watched as his sister lingered in the shadows of a young moonlight. She watched as Victor's coven glided up over the wall. She snuck into the city under the veil of slaughter that her brother's coven provided. The scent of blood was strong through the air, and Victor's coven of three dozen strong crippled the forces of Astra' Kandra with ease. It wasn't until a pair of celestial beings appeared did Lilith rise from the shadows. Two angels, dressed in the finest armor and wielding the finest swords, cut through Victor's coven with tremendous ease. Lilith clawed at the angels and tore away at their bright, shining skin. The angels cried as their divine blood was shed from their open skin. They danced and twirled, taking on Lilith's flank. Their swords cut across Lilith's body, but the daughter of Satan was quick to disperse into shadow. She danced with the angels and fought through the night until one of the holy weapons connected with her backside.

A flower bloomed from the ashes of eternity and then, like a tear of lightning streaking across the sky, Victor awoke to the real-world cries of his sister's distant death. Lilith's scream seeped into the wooden casket and sliced through Victor's flesh and mind. It served to awaken something within the vampire's heartless chest. Burning with a shadowy flame, Victor bolted his eyes open.

Part Eight
Exquisite Blood

Bursting from the coffin in a fit of rage, Victor's fury was met by absolute silence. The coffin's wooden planks splintered and fractured across an empty room. There was no welcome party to be had. There were no men with bright armor and light-infused weapons waiting for him. There were no priests welding crosses and holy water, all the while wearing their condescending smile, nor were there any angels with glittering skin standing beside the door with holy swords drawn. The mortuary was empty of life and only the dead were company to the son of Satan.

Victor's chest felt tight. He was breathing heavily and his face reflected a deep yet silent rage. His anger seethed from his pale skin as he lifted himself up into the air and floated across the room. He closed his eyes and called out in silence to his chosen. He could see through their eyes. They were springing from the shadows of concealment and racing towards the city gate. They shrieked and cried as they ran forward - the war cry of the vampire coven.

Victor opened his eyes and withdrew Heart Cutter from its sheath. The blade sliced through the air with a sharp, chaotic ambient cry as it was drawn. Victor began scanning his surroundings. A naked body lie still across a wooden table, and the low-lit light of a flame danced from within a lamp beside the corpse. Someone was working on embalming the corpse just moments before Victor rose from his coffin.

The morgue's entrance had been left open and a cool draft wafted into the room. The moonlight beyond trickled in and Victor continued to glide towards the exit. Victor stopped beneath the lunar shine. The light brightened his pale face. His expression was twisted and sour. His eyes were bleeding with darkness as he scanned through the barren streets of the legendary town. He could hear a commotion off in the distance. No doubt it was the aftermath: high tensions and paranoia that ensued following the slaughtering of his sister.

A great bell began to sound from the city's watch along the wall. Victor forced a smirk. His children had come home to roost.

Heart Cutter began to whisper thoughts of hunger unto Victor.

"Yes," the vampire said softly. "I can smell it, too."

The scent of fear was rife through the air. It only made blood taste sweeter, and both he and his blade hungered.

"Put it down," a voice called out from Victor's right-hand side.

The vampire's booted feet kissed the cobblestone road. He slowly lowered Heart Cutter to his side and turned to face the man who had given the command.

"They said that you'd come at night," the man spoke from beneath the veil of Venetian mystique mask. The guise was silver and covered the man's entire face. A blue peacock lined the right-hand side of the mask. Victor couldn't be certain, but it seemed as though the fake bird slithered and moved as the man spoke. "But for you to walk right into my hands... what are the fucking odds?"

More bells could be heard sounding in the distance. Hidden between the strikes was a tune of a very different nature, one that Victor was keen to take note of. The masked man's heart was thumping through his chest. He seemed calm, but the organ told a different story. It was young and fierce, and Heart Cutter tugged against the vampire's arm as it hungered.

The man was wearing a black cloak and holding a crossbow with both of his hands. The weapon's string was pulled back and a bolt was loaded: ready to fire.

Victor smirked and let go of Heart Cutter. The weapon sailed through the air towards the masked man. The hunter then pulled the trigger on his crossbow and a bolt was released. It sliced cleanly through Victor's belly. A strange burning sensation tore through Victor's insides and he yelped as he keeled over and clenched the wound. The hunter dropped his crossbow and threw back his tunic. A collection of daggers and chained crosses hung from his chest. He was quick to withdraw a sword from his waist and pluck a flailed cross from his vest. Heart Cutter was foolish in going directly forward. The man deflected the blow and Victor's weapon was flung high up into the air. Heart Cutter twirled for a moment and then came to a dead stop in the sky. It whistled as it descended back down to the earth with an unnatural speed and unholy desire.

In a delicate dance, the man spun and lashed out at Victor with the cross, all the while using his sword to deflect the blows from Victor's spirit weapon.

Victor flared his upper lip and exposed his teeth as he dodged the blows from the cross-shaped flail. He was still clenching his side. The burning sensation ran deep, and Victor could only assume that the arrow's tip had been coated in a holy water residue.

Heart Cutter clinked and scraped against the man's sword while Victor continued to dodge the strikes made against him. The masked assassin dropped his flail and then wrapped a second hand around his broadsword. He channeled ferocity in deflecting another blow from Heart Cutter. This time, Victor's weapon was discarded towards a stone wall. The blade's tip sunk into the stone as the man released a hand from his own blade and plucked a cross-shaped dagger from his vest. He threw the small blade at Victor, but the vampire was quick to blink forward and to the side. The man followed through with a twirling swing of his blade and Victor bled further away.

The vampire's eyes grew wide. He had been cornered with his back to a wall. The man had played him well, and in a final swing, he brought down a taste of God's might channeled behind a weapon infused with holy magic. The cross-shaped flail smashed cleanly across Victor's cheek. Blood, muscle, and bone spewed from his face and he yelped as a bright light erupted from the weapon's point of impact. The light crept and burned across Victor's skin like a web of veins. The vampire squealed, hunched over and cupping his broken face.

Victor had been a cocky fool. His sister had warned him of the great challenge he'd face. She had told him that only their father's rage could escort him safely through the city, and he had failed to heed her warning.

The bright light of the masked assailant's glowing weapon pulsed from within his grasp. Victor considered his sister's sacrifice. She had died at the hands of mortal men wielding divine magic. He considered for a moment his own fate. Had he traveled all this way, just to fall at the hands of a single man?

Victor lowered his hands and lifted his broken face. Loose flesh hung from open wounds along his cheek. He hissed as the man stepped forward to finish him off. Cornered like a sinner facing devils and demons, Victor was desperate for options. He leapt forward towards the assailant with his claws stretched outwards. Hissing and screaming, his attack was cut short as the flail connected with his left shoulder. Bones cracked and Victor's left arm went limp. Still, he nipped and clawed at the attacker. He cut through leather straps and chainmail. His desperation featured into doubt, and then something unexpected happened.

The man dropped his flail and froze in place. The dulcet tones of his vocal cords struggling against the weight of Death's nagging pull lingered in the midnight air. Warm blood rained down upon Victor, and the vampire lifted his broken face to find the tip of a sword had pierced cleanly through the man's chest.

Heart Cutter, Victor thought with a hazy mind.

The man dropped to his knees, choking on blood beneath his steel mask. He then fell forward into the dirt with Victor's sword hanging from his backside.

Victor leaned forward and wrapped his fingers around the edge of the mask. He tugged at the veil, but it didn't come off. He pressed his lips against an exposed area of flesh beneath the mask. Crippled by his wounds, Victor parted his dry lips and fed on the man's warm blood. He drained the dying man and restored his own sense of vitality. The wounds along his face healed and his arm regained its strength.

With his strength restored, Victor planted a booted foot against the man's motionless chest. The crosses on his vest hissed from beneath the weight of Victor's foot. He then lifted himself into the air and pulled harder at the mask. The wet noise of tearing flesh bled out across the courtyard. Victor lifted the mask. The man's lifeless face had been torn open. Blue eyes gazed up at Victor from bloody sockets. The skin had been welded to the mask, and it had also been torn off with it. The red, skinless meat that had been left behind made the deceased man unidentifiable.

Victor looked at the mask for a moment. The veil was of lightweight cast iron design. Victor assumed that the peacock was a tell of an order of sorts, but he couldn't quite understand who this man had been or how he had known of Victor and Lilith's arrival. He didn't care. The thought of Lilith forced Victor to return his attention to the task at hand. He flared his upper lip in anger and discarded the mask. He then placed his palm against the end of Heart Cutter's hilt. The weapon was motionless, suspended in the grasp of total euphoria and bliss. Victor slid his hand along the hilt and wrapped his fingers around the handle. He tugged at the blade, but the weapon's hold on the dead man's heart was true. Victor had no time for games. He forcefully withdrew the blood-soaked weapon from the dead man's chest. Heart Cutter cried out in animosity as it was removed from its meal and slipped into its sheath. Victor then turned his gaze back towards the streets.

Curious faces, lit by candles, took to frost covered windows and peered out at Victor as he levitated through the street and began to make way for the city's holy sector.

Soldiers and guards were quick to race towards the wall and bell towers. They had been summoned to defend the entrance against an onslaught of Victor's coven. In the hours and day leading up to the city's besiegement, his followers had gone out and multiplied. The distraction at the gate had served its purpose well. The son of Satan was already within the city's walls, and he was en route towards his prize. It wasn't until Victor approached the Golden Arch of Maithal did soldiers begin to take note of the vampire.

"Halt!" A knight ordered. He was standing with another beneath the archway. A tarnished road of silver lie beneath their feet. This served to be the entrance into the city's holy sector. Ariel's sanctum lie at the heart of the district, and Victor could smell the lingering presence of a divine soul. She wasn't here, but she had been, and Victor could taste it. "I said halt!" The knight repeated in a stern tone.

Victor smiled and six vampires lept out from the shadows. Shrieking and screaming, they pounced on one of the men and quickly drove him to the ground. His metal armor scraped across the silver stone as Victor's followers fought to claw and tear at his face. He kicked and screamed, but within minutes his body went limp and he was left lying still in a pool of his own blood.

The second soldier was frozen in time. Suspended within the grasp of total shock and fear, he was paralyzed, staring into Victor's dark eyes.

The six remaining members of Victor's new coven approached and knelt before their master. They silently offered this sacrifice of blood, but Victor had no time to feed. He wordlessly whispered into the minds of his followers as he stepped under the archway and approached the surviving knight. He crept closer to the man's face and whispered something incoherent into his ear. He broke the man's will with ease. The knight plucked off his helmet, revealing a head of golden hair and prickly, unshaven skin.

"Turn him," Victor instructed of his coven. "He is to take an alternate route to the sanctum," he added before disengaging and continuing forward into the holy district. The squeals of the man could be heard behind Victor as his coven took turns feeding from the man's neck. The six vampires then rose up into the air and took off to follow behind their master.

This is all that's left, Victor thought of his clan. Three dozen strong had been reduced to a number of six vampires. Now six plus one, it would be enough. It had to be.

"By the power of *Christ*!" A pair of bald-headed priests - dressed in white linens and fine jewelry - shouted as they leapt out from an unlit alleyway. They had vials of water in their hands and they were attempting to throw the holy bombs at Victor.

Victor's followers were quick to pounce on the attackers. They tore at their linens, bellies, and chests. They spilled blood across the silver road. The vials of holy water shattered on the ground. The water smelled of fire, and Victor twitched his upper lip in disgust. Above all else, he was disappointed in the overall lack of effort. Perhaps his sister and coven had done more damage to the city's ranks than he had anticipated. Surely Lilith didn't go down without a fight.

A golden steeple could be seen towering among the city skyline. It stuck out from the rest of the simplistic buildings. Constructed with fine, warped steel, the sanctum was a gateway to heaven: the portal where Ariel was said to be found.

The coven of six escorted Victor through the holy sector. They would catch fleeing civilians and silence their cries with bloodshed. Victor didn't have to lift a finger. His followers were without mind. Obedient and ruthless, they murdered anyone and everyone foolish enough to be out in the streets on this night of conquest.

The sound of steel boots clicked through the air. From the side streets, a quarter-dozen knights bled out onto the silver walkway ahead. They were dressed from head to toe in plate mail that brightly shone - even without the presence of a sun in the sky. The soldiers were well equipped. From broadswords to scimitars, shields, flails, maces, and spears, each of the knights were seasoned in the ways of war.

Victor smirked. *At last, a challenge*, he thought. He lifted his hands in the air as he continued to glide forward along the path and his six followers screamed with the war cry of the allfather below as they leapt forward and sprinted towards their prey.

The soldiers shouted a series of commands and then shuffled closer towards one another. They had taken a defensive position and were waiting for the coven to arrive.

Victor withdrew Heart Cutter. The blade's hilt vibrated within the palm of his hand. It's desire to feed was ever constant. His coven collided with the line of soldiers. They shrieked over the sound of flesh being battered and torn. Although they outnumbered the soldiers, they lacked weapons or armor, and the knights were quick to best them in combat. Viscera littered the ground around the soldier's defensive line, but only one of Victor's six had fallen. The rest were injured badly. Their skin was littered from head to toe with mortal wounds, but they had been gifted with something that couldn't be found on the mortal plane. Through Victor's pact with the reaper, his followers were promised to Death, and that meant that they could only be stopped by means of total evisceration. They continued to scrape and tear at the soldiers.

A second member of the coven fell to the ground. The vampire had been split cleanly into two halves. His legs went limp, but his upper torso was still alive and well. His insides bled from out his open chest, but still he clawed towards the soldiers, wearing the look of insanity and lust in his eyes.

Victor suppressed the urge to cackle. These children were pawns to a cause that they could never truly understand. Even with their rank of insignificance, they had proven themselves useful accessories in murder and conquest.

A flash of lightning struck the tip of the golden spire beyond and a radiant blaze ruptured from the basin of the tower. Victor was forced to shield his face from the intensity of the light. He could hear the muffled cries of his coven. The sounds were drenched by a cleansing thunder that tore through the air like the tides of a great storm come ashore. Heart Cutter sang in his hands. The steel grew red-hot, and Victor was forced to drop the blade as he continued to shield his face.

The flash of light was brief yet divine. It burned at the skin along Victor's arms. He slowly unmasked his face. The scent of sulfur and brimstone lingered. The remaining members of his coven had been reduced to ash, and a faint glow was lit ablaze at the basin of the nearby spire.

The child of Satan had breached the holy city's walls with ease. Through murder and defile, he had pushed inwards towards the holy sanctum. Countless lives had been stolen at the hands of his sister, himself, and his coven. Now, the gatekeeper Ariel had arrived to defend what was left.

Part Nine
Force of Will

Three plated warriors remained standing between Victor and the spire. The ashes of his coven, dispersed into the wind with the aftershock of Ariel's arrival, sung tribute to Victor's impending defeat. The divine soldiers were hunched over in a defensive position wielding both shields and spears. They advanced like a wall of steel, their boots clicking loudly against the surface of the silver road.

With his arms to his side, Victor opened his right hand. Heart Cutter rose from the ground and found its way back into its master's palm. Victor's upper lip twitched as he clenched his grip and flew forward. His weapon clanked off the soldier's shields. They extended their spears and Victor was quick to dodge the predictable strikes. He released his grip on Heart Cutter and the unholy weapon continued to drive with a series of swipes. Victor rose further into the air and then blinked behind the soldiers.

Before they had time to spin around and confront the vampire's now flanking position, Victor sunk his nails into the backside of one of their necks. The area of exposed flesh was quick to split and tear beneath his feral grip. The knight crumbled to the ground with a muffled cry, and one of the two remaining soldiers spun around to confront their flank.

Victor withdrew his hand from the fallen warrior. His fingers were covered in warm blood. He lifted the hand to his face and inhaled the savory scent. He then wrapped his lips around his fingers and closed his eyes. He let out a moan as he reveled in a moment of total bliss. He could hear the horrific screams of a second knight falling at the hands of Heart Cutter. The unholy weapon never tired.

A spear impaled Victor and he coughed out a mouthful of blood as he reopened his eyes. The single remaining knight had struck the vampire cleanly through the belly. Victor chuckled as he wrapped his free hand around the spear and pulled his way closer to the warrior. The fighter's eyes grew wide with fright as he watched the vampire climb closer along the weapon's shaft. The knight then released his grip on the weapon and withdrew a mace from his side. Before he could lash out and strike at Victor, Heart Cutter punctured cleanly through the holy warrior's backside. It pierced straight through the man's beating heart. Victor's face was showered in blood. He looked directly into the man's dying eyes as his lifeforce faded into the twilight.

Victor smirked as the lifeless knight dropped to the ground. He withdrew the spear from his belly. The sound of someone groaning through a congestion of broken bones and total pain reverberated from below. Victor glanced down at a heap of trembling steel. The man with the broken neck squirmed on the ground like a slug drenched in salt. He was twisting and gagging, all the while holding his gauntlet to his neck. Victor hushed the man's agony and peeled back the gloved hands to gaze upon his work. The neck was twisted and mangled badly. He pressed his nose to the flesh and then sunk his teeth in to feed. The man kicked his feet like a fish out of water against the line of damnation. His fate would now belong to the vampire.

"Victor!" A feminine voice called from behind the vampire.

Victor froze like a cat caught devouring the corpse of a fresh kill. His eyes shimmered with darkness as he caroused in the ecstasy of the moment.

"It is over!" The woman added.

Victor discarded his price and turned to greet his guest.

The guardian angel, Ariel, was standing two blocks down the silver-lined road. She stood tall with blonde hair that flowed freely in the air behind her. She had great, angelic wings that hung from her sides, and she was dressed in a collection of white linens and golden plate mail. Her skin radiated with a soft, warm glow. The scent of the divine blood coursing through her veins was intoxicating, and Victor's jaw began to slowly drop as the irises of his eyes dilated. He savored over the thought of sinking his fangs into her beautiful skin and leeching the divine being of her celestial blood. He wouldn't waste a drop.

"You have come for me!" She cried.

"I have," Victor moaned softly with a smirk. He was losing his sense of self to the prospect of tasting what she stored beneath her skin.

"So come and take me!" She commanded.

Victor squinted his eyes and gritted his teeth. The offer felt sexual, and the promise of ravaging this divine creature - leeching her of lifeforce - was painfully tempting. It was a thought that tugged at his core with the might of total addiction. Despite this, he was here with purpose, and so he extended a hand into the air. Heart Cutter rose up from the fallen corpse that it fed upon and rested its hilt within Victor's open palm. Victor then clenched tightly before placing his free hand along the cusp of his father's broken rib.

Ariel lifted her wings into the air. She extended them and a circle of dust was blown away from where she stood. With the wings now drawn out, she further exuded a sense of beauty that was unmatched by any mortal or devil alike. Her lack of expression left her appearing helpless, but Victor knew better than to underestimate one of God's chosen.

Ariel pulled back her wings and then fluttered them forward, standing mightily still on the ground. A gale of wind bursted through the air. Victor was tossed up like a fly to a storm. He tumbled and spun and grunted and cursed before slamming into a stone wall. Rocks and debris served to entomb him as a wall crumbled under the weight of his impact. He was left lying broken beneath the heap of rubble.

"Your mind is a slave to your father's will, child," the angel spoke softly. Her voice was muffled by the tomb, and yet still it was soothing like the mist of an early morning fog.

Heart Cutter rose from the debris and pulled Victor to his feet. Once standing, the vampire plucked his father's broken rib from his leather belt. He hissed in anger at how insignificant the guardian had made him feel in tossing him to the wind. After all of this bloodshed, he had reached the angel, and the prophecy of his destiny was to be fulfilled on this morning. He released his grip on the weapon and Heart Cutter sailed through the air towards the guardian angel.

Ariel drew her sword from its sheath.

"There is a great truth that you do not see," she called.

Ariel's weapon was glowing from hilt to tip with a fierce, golden blaze. She placed the palm of her free hand flush along the weapon's fuller. She then twirled forward and slashed diagonally. Her strike connected with Heart Cutter. Despite the spirit weapon's unholy speed, she had deflected the blow with relative ease. Victor's weapon hissed as Ariel's pulsed with light and a sharp shriek tore through the air as Heart Cutter was split into two separate halves. The broken sword fell to the ground and the spirit of Keshmesh was released, howling into the midnight air.

Ariel's method of swordplay was beautifully elegant. Much like the waltz of an estranged lover come to a ball on the eve of total courtship, her movements were calculated and laced with a gentle splendor backed by total virtue. Her strike had been wonderfully swift and eminently powerful.

Victor's eyes softened as he watched the spirit of Keshmesh

dissipate into the air. His broken blade remained still against the ground. It was little more than useless steel now. Wounded and unarmed, Victor looked to the ground for a weapon. He kept hold of his father's fragment and dove for a nearby spear. Twirling to his feet, he launched the spear at the guardian and blinked closer towards her. Ariel stepped to the right and dodged the ranged strike. Victor had inched his way closer to her, but the gap between them was still significant. She again bellowed a gust of wind from her wings and Victor was rendered motionless in the air before falling back down to the earth.

Just as defeat was creeping ever closer into the son's mind, he caught a whiff of a familiar fragrance. The scent was of fresh pine, and it forced Victor to widen his eyes and reel his head, for there were no pine trees to be found within all the city.

A heap of shadow hissed out into the street. The shroud of darkness then imploded in on itself, forming into the shape of a humanoid silhouette.

Lilith? Victor thought, shocked to think that his sister could somehow be alive.

As the darkness faded, Lilith was left standing alongside her brother. Her body was lacerated and torn from head to toe. Her face was littered with tears across her soft, beautiful skin, and her clothes had been shredded down to bits and scraps that only covered her waist and thighs.

"Sister..." Victor was at a loss for words.

Much like Victor, Lilith's breathing had become boisterous and heavy. She was trying to inhale air with lungs that were filled with liquid and blood. She could barely stand, but she remained at her brother's side, wearing the ferocity and will of their father. She glared at the guardian angel and growled softly between bloated and battered lips.

Ariel released her free hand from the edge of her divine weapon. "You surround yourself with your father's servants," she gestured forward with the tip of her sword. "This darkness only serves to further blind you, child."

"Do not listen to her," Lilith wheezed. "They are losing and grow desperate in their hour of defeat."

Ariel pressed her freehand to an item that hung by her waist side.

"The trumpet of Christ Risen," Lilith seethed. "We must silence her... *now*!"

Together and as one, the two siblings bursted forward. Their speed was unmatched by neither light nor sound. They flanked both sides of the guardian and began to claw at the angel. Ariel spun around and severed one of Lilith's hands at the forearm. Lilith screamed as Victor managed to connect with his strikes and tear away at the angel's backside. He used his claws and his father's rib fragment as weapons, for it was all that he had. A heap of crimson-stained feathers drifted to the ground. The plumes ignited into a fiery blaze as they kissed the earth. The three of them were devoured in flames as the fight ensued. Victor continued to tear at Ariel's wings until only bloody stumps remained. The angel had kept her backside to Victor while she did her best to keep both of the attackers at bay. With the wings gone, Victor believed that he had a shot at lodging his Father's bone fragment into the guardian's belly. He repositioned his grip on the shard just as Ariel severed Lilith's second forearm. Ariel kicked Lilith in the chest and sent the daughter flying back into a nearby building.

Victor leapt through the fire and lunged for the angel's side. Ariel spun around and kneed Victor's arm before following through with a strike of her sword that cut cleanly across his chest. The vampire dropped to his knees and staggered in place. Ariel had been crippled by exhaustion and her wounds were countless, but she still stood. Her presence towered, and Victor was left feeling small before her wake.

Both Victor and Ariel looked deeply into one another's eyes. Unspoken words were exchanged. This was the end, and despite all the work, all the bloodshed, murder and chaos, God would win.

It was then that a forgotten asset emerged. One of the three knights, left to turn, had been stripped of his fate and was now servant to the son. The ball of his bladed mace crashed into

Ariel's side and the divine creature crumpled. She shrieked in agony as the hefty hunk of metal was pulled out from her side. She forced herself back up and twirled around to cleave the man's head cleanly from his neck. She then lost her balance and dropped to one knee. Lilith burst forward from the smoldering pile of debris. She pounced on Ariel's back, but without hands, she was left with only her teeth to tear at the angel's face with.

Victor tried to woozily stand. Ariel dropped her weapon and tapped into her remaining reservoir of strength. She exerted herself beyond limit in order to dismount her rider. Lilith was discarded and thrown into her brother. The two siblings collapsed into a pile of rubble. Ariel swayed before them. Blood pouring from every inch of her skin, she pressed the trumpet to her lips and crashed to her knees.

"No!" Lilith growled, choking on a mouthful of blood.

Ariel used the last of her strength to blow on the instrument. The tune vibrated across the lands and an eerie song of divinity was channeled through the trumpet's horn. The clouds above parted to reveal the heavens above. A white fire then streamed down from the sky.

The divine storm that bled from the clouds was breathtaking. The fire's reflection could be seen across the watery surface of Victor's swollen eyes. There was no time to flee and there was no counter to be had. The moment of his demise was striking down from the heavens like lightning. Soon, he'd be cast back down to hell. He'd be left to face his father with nothing but failure and defeat. He'd be stripped of all honor and titles; perhaps even discarded to the pools of anguish for his insolvency and left to suffer at the hands of torment for the rest of eternity.

With utter annihilation creeping ever closer, Lilith burst into shadow. In her gaseous form, she encased her brother in a veil of darkness. Hissing and screaming, she shielded Victor from the strike of holy fire. Victor was left suspended in a bubble of chaos as the collision of light and dark tore at the fabrics of reality all around him. He listened as his sister was vaporized at the hands of such raw power. Her screams were eternal, and spacetime was warped under the weight of the combustion.

With this slit in reality, time had been fragmented and moved slower than it should. The dust fell and Victor was left lying on the ground. He gazed up at the tear in the sky. It shone brightly with a meager glimpse into the heavens above. Victor lowered his gaze. Ariel lie across from him. She was missing an eye, but using the one that she still had to stare directly into the face of the son. Victor spotted his father's bone fragment lying beside her.

The loss of his sister drove Victor to empathy and anger. His animosity only served to shatter his mind at the will of his father's hidden hand. Victor's eyes swirled in pools of darkness and he channeled his fury into strength so that he could pull himself closer to the guardian. His broken face was further splitting under the weight of a forgotten sense of self. He exposed and flared his teeth as he began to drool, clawing ever closer towards the guardian angel. Ariel failed in standing and instead watched helplessly as Victor grabbed hold of the nearby bone fragment.

Victor would change the course of history. He would dismiss the prophets as false. He would fulfill his own destiny, prove himself to his father, and be known as the son who brought down heaven.

"The will of all things is ultimately their own," Ariel choked out with her final hold on life. The sun was beginning to rise behind her. She was dying, and it was now that the blade must be plunged into her womb as to impregnate her before she ascended into heaven. Her divine words snared Victor and he stuttered in place for a moment, the tip of the shard pressed to her broken belly. "It doesn't belong to Satan, nor does it belong to God. You are free to do as you wish."

With the phrase, Victor's sense of rage and anger, lust and drive was washed away like mud from a rock cast to sea. The darkness in his eyes faded and he looked upon the broken angel with an expression of confusion and shock. His hand twitched and he released his grip on the bone fragment. He then watched as Ariel's soul rose up from her corpse and ascended into the heavens above.

The tear in the sky remained, and Victor was left kneeling in the center of a city beseeched by both heaven and hell. Bodies and blood, wreckage and debris littered the city streets as the sun climbed higher over the distant horizon.

Victor clamored to his feet. He could barely stand. He watched with battered eyes as God's golden rays tore across the landscape. Just before dawn could break over the fabled city sky, Victor disappeared into the withering night. He set out to live in hiding: clinging ever further to the secrets and shadows of the exotic mortal plane.

www.ingramcontent.com/pod-product-compliance
Lightning Source LLC
LaVergne TN
LVHW051016080826
845145LV00009B/2649